A Key to English Grammar Practice

Raj N Bakshi

Orient Longman

ORIENT LONGMAN PRIVATE LIMITED

Registered Office
3-6-752 Himayatnagar, Hyderabad 500 029 (A.P.), India
Email: cogeneral@orientlongman.com

Other Offices
Bangalore, Bhopal, Bhubaneshwar, Chennai
Ernakulam, Guwahati, Hyderabad, Jaipur, Kolkata
Lucknow, Mumbai, New Delhi, Patna

First Published 2006

ISBN 81 250 3004 2

Typeset in Times 10/12 by
OSDATA
Hyderabad

Printed in India at
Orion Printers Private Limited
Hyderabad 500 004

Published by
Orient Longman Private Limited
3-6-752, Himayatnagar,
Hyderabad 500 029.
Email: hyd2_ollhyd@sancharnet.in

Unit 1

Exercise 1. *(The words before the slash/comprise the subject and the words after the slash/indicate the predicate.)* 1. Her younger brother/is a famous doctor. 2. The Finance Minister/has given us tax concession. 3. Meena/runs very fast. 4. The food/smells very good. 5. All the old employees/are unhappy. 6. Her teachers/consider her witty. 7. Rajneesh/is sitting in the corner. 8. The Board's decision/ has made us happy. 9. The University/has framed a new rule. 10. The old students/have gone out for dinner. 11. Monica/offered Ashok her car yesterday. 12. The tall boy standing in the corner/is our captain. 13. He/has grown tall. 14. That blue car/is very old. 15. All the students/sang well at the party. 16. Her father/works in a bank. 17. My cousin/looked splendid at the party. 18. All the girls/watched TV in the evening. 19. Lions/roar. 20. Krishna/bought a briefcase yesterday.

Exercise 2. 1. Our college (S) begins (Intrv) in July (A). 2. They (S) play (Intrv) while their parents are away (A). 3. Gita (S) writes (Intrv) with a pen (A). 4. The children (S) slept (Intrv) till 10' clock (A) yesterday (A). 5. Vijay and Suresh (S) run (Intrv) whenever they see a dog (A). 6. The train (S) arrived (Intrv) late (A). 7. I (S) slept (Intrv) there (A). 8. Soldiers (S) rest (Intrv) when they are on leave (A). 9. She (S) ran (Intrv) fast (A). 10. I (S) jumped (Intrv) over the wall (A). 11. Babies (S) cry (Intrv) loudly (A). 12. The boy (S) studied (Intrv) in the room (A). 13. Asha (S) slipped (Intrv) on the ice (A). 14. Salma (S) sleeps (Intrv) on the mat (A). 15. The bombs (S) exploded (Intrv) continuously (A).

Exercise 3. 1. The boys (S) were (LV) busy (CS). 2. The Indians (S) were (LV) the winners (CS). 3. Her brother (S) is (LV) a fool (CS). 4. The examination (S) will be (LV) on Tuesday (CS). 5. My neighbour (S) is (LV) tall (CS). 6. The meeting (S) is (LV) at 4.30 (CS). 7. The policeman (S) may be (LV) right (CS). 8. Her father (S) is (LV) a doctor (CS). 9. Lal Bhadur Shastri (S) was (LV) a great leader (CS). 10. Jane (S) is (LV) talented (CS). 11. The boys (S) were (LV) in the field (CS). 12. The party (S) must have been (LV) enjoyable (CS). 13. My mother (S) is (LV) upstairs (CS). 14. They (S) were (LV) in the library (CS). 15. Manoj (S) is (LV) an architect (CS).

Exercise 4. Amitabh (S) appeared (LV) happy (CS). 2. The music (S) sounded (LV) strange (CS). 3. They (S) feel (LV) annoyed CS). 4. My brother (S) became (LV) a professor (CS). 5. Monisha (S) looks (LV) happy (CS). 6. Rekha (S) seemed (LV) sad (CS). 7. This dog (S) seems (LV) restless (CS). 8. The rose (S) smells (LV) sweet (CS). 9. This fruit (S) tastes (LV) bitter (CS). 10 He (S) remained (LV) the captain (CS).

Unit 2

Exercise 1. 1. Shailaja (S) has taken (Trv) my cycle (Od). 2. Her father (S) has been (LV) ill (CS). 3. I (S) need (Trv) a coat (Od). 4. My coat (S) is (LV) warm (CS). 5. Your wife (S) is standing (Intrv) outside (Adv). 6. She (S) met (Trv) the director (Od) yesterday (Adv). 7. My friend (S) visits (Trv) me (Od) every Sunday (Adv). 8. She (S) slept (Intrv) in the morning (Adv). 9. Your skirt (S) looks (LV) very pretty (CS). 10. They (S) have started (Trv) the game (Od). 11. John (S) has been (LV) a university professor (CS) for five years (Adv). 12. She (S) boarded (Trv) the train (Od) with her luggage (Adv). 13. The man (S) polished (Trv) the car (Od) on Friday (Adv). 14. The car (S) turned (Intrv) sharply (Adv). 15. The Principal (S) delivered (Trv) the speech (Od) in the hall (Adv). 16. Rita (S) looked (LV) unhappy (CS) at the party (Adv). 17. The policeman (S) carried (Trv) his rifle (Od) on his shoulder (Adv). 18. I (S) bought (Trv) this book (Od) in Delhi (Adv). 19. She (S) followed (Trv) him (Od) everywhere (Adv). 20. The leader of the opposition (S) criticised (Trv) the government (Od) at the press conference (Adv).

Exercise 2. 1. My daughter (S) attends (Trv) Delhi Public School (Od). 2. The grocer (S) is weighing (Trv) tea leaves (Od). 3. She (S) told (Trv) us (Oi) a story (Od) every night (Adv). 4. The Principal (S) granted (Trv) him (Oi) leave (Od) on Monday (Adv). 5. The goalkeeper (S) caught (Trv) the ball (Od) with his hands (Adv). 6. Mohit (S) asked (Trv) Seema (Oi) difficult questions (Od) during the interview (Adv), or Seema (S) asked (Trv) Mohit (Oi) difficult questions (Od) during the interview (Adv). 7. I (S) have purchased (Trv) this house (Od) recently (Adv). 8. They (S) have paid (Trv) us (Oi) the rent (Od). 9. Mukesh (S) painted (Trv) this picture (Od) last month (Adv). 10. Meenakshi (S) has lent (Trv) me (Oi) her car (Od). 11. The shop assistant (S) paid (Trv) us (Oi) the receipt (Od) after we paid the money (Adv). 12. The gardener (S) planted (Trv) flowers (Od) in the garden (Adv). 13. Mr Kapoor (S) teaches (Trv) us (Oi) English (Od). 14. We (S) collected (Trv) our son's report card (Od) in the morning (Adv). 15. Mrs Soni (S) served (Trv) us (Oi) tea (Od) in the evening (Adv).

Exercise 3. My father gave a book to me. 2. Radha sent a box of biscuits to her brother. 3. My mother bought a bicycle for me. 4. Mr Sharma wrote a letter to us. 5. He found a house for her. 6. Shyam paid the money to me.

Exercise 4. 1. We reported the matter to the police. 2. Shabana introduced me to her husband, or Shabana introduced her husband to me. 3. She admitted her fault to her mother. 4. She suggested it to me.

5. He confessed his crime to the police. 6. You should not mention it to anyone. 7. He declared his income to the Income Tax officer. 8. Can you describe your plan to us? 9. You can tell me whatever you want. 10. He explained his plan to the committee.

Exercise 5. 1. That girl (S) is (LV) our college captain (Cs). 2. Seema (S) sliced (Trv) the potatoes (Od) with a knife (Adv). 3. They (S) made (Trv) her (Od) the captain of the hockey team (Co). 4. The chair (S) was lying (Intrv) in the centre (Adv). 5. The milk (S) has turned (LV) sour (Cs). 6. She (S) opened (Trv) the door (Od) with a key (Adv). 7. Our director (S) made (Trv) us (Od) comfortable (Co) during the meeting (Adv). 8. Her parents (S) called (Trv) her (Od) Susie (Co). 9. The faculty (S) presented (Trv) her (Oi) a watch (Od) on her birthday (Adv). 10. Rajesh (S) bought (Trv) his son (Oi) a cycle (Od). 11. Her sister (S) has been (LV) a dancer (Cs) for several years (Adv). 12. The car (S) turned (Intrv) left (Adv) on the bridge (Adv). 13. They (S) built (Trv) her (Oi) a house (Od). 14. The Prime Minister (S) considered (Trv) the experiment (Od) a success (Co). 15. That building (S) is (LV) very impressive (Cs). 16. Her father (S) has been (LV) an army officer (Cs) for fifteen years (Adv). 17. My mother (S) hit (Trv) the ball (Od) with a stick (Adv). 18. The Principal (S) made (Trv) Varinder (Od) the monitor of the class (Co) yesterday (Adv). 19. The plane (S) landed (Intrv) at the Delhi airport (Adv) at 2 o'clock (Adv). 20. They (S) chose (Trv) Alka (Od) their leader (Cs) at the meeting (Adv).

Exercise 6. *(The following sentences are only possible answers).* 1. a) She is sleeping. b) Mukesh is studying. 2. a) Nandini's mother is a doctor. b) Sushil and Vinod are pilots. 3. a) He has bought a cricket bat. b) My mother is cooking dinner. 4. a) The management allotted Rohini a new house. b) The Principal gave Mr Nair a computer. 5. a) The management appointed Rohini the chairperson. b) The Principal appointed Mr Nair the hostel warden. 6. a) They are playing in the garden. b) She is sleeping on the floor. 7. Kunal's father has been a teacher for ten years. b) She has been an invalid for two months. 8. a) My grandfather constructed this house in 1960. b) Rita gave me this book yesterday. 9. a) My mother bought me a shirt yesterday. b) The Director asked him an easy question during the interview. 10. a) The Chief Minister appointed Mr Singh a Cabinet Minister last week. b) His statement made her angry just as she was going to deliver the speech.

Exercise 7. *(The following sentences are only possible answers).* 1. My brother purchased this building last month. 2. Sunita is talented. 3. Arnaz wrote a novel last year. 4. Our dog killed a rat. 5. My father has been a surgeon for years. 6. We attended the party immediately. 7. His father has planted mango trees in the garden. 8. The girls are laughing loudly. 9. Samson worked in the garden yesterday. 10. The car turned right. 11. Samir called Rohan a liar. 12. Our English teacher considers Rahul very intelligent. 13. The team chose Peter the secretary in the sports room. 14. Madhuri looked very colourful at the wedding. 15. The General Manager considers him intelligent. 16. Rakesh gave Meera a diamond necklace on her birthday. 17. Feroz and Sanjay are policemen. 18. Mita and Kunal wrote fast. 19. Monisha appears happy. 20. All of us consider him naïve.

Unit 3

Exercise 1. 1. Lions are very powerful. 2. Trees give us shade. 3. Cows are domestic animals. 4. Sparrows are birds. 5. Aeroplanes land at airports. 6. Mangoes are delicious fruits. 7. Babies drink milk. 8. Men or women can apply for this post/these posts. 9. Tables and chairs can be made of wood. 10. Dogs are faithful animals. 11. Tigers run fast. 12. Whales are mammals. 13. Deer are very timid. 14. Trains can go faster than cars. 15. Apples are good for health. 16. Monica keeps her cars in her garage/garages. 17. Fish live in water. 18. Athletes need good diet. 19. My brothers visited my uncles yesterday. 20. Chemists sell medicines. 21. The policemen have caught the thieves. 22. My sisters are pilots. 23. Pilots fly aeroplanes. 24. Authors write novels. 25. Children like playing.

Exercise 2. 1. My cousin is a hockey player. 2. A nightingale sings well. 3. We have a dog and a duck at home. 4. A child must drink milk. 5. A car is made of steel. 6. There is a jackal in this field. 7. A snake can be dangerous. 8. An egg is good for health. 9. A donkey is an animal. 10. A tiger is ferocious. 11. A monkey is intelligent. 12. I met a beautiful girl at the party. 13. A bird flies in the sky. 14. A lion is a strong animal. 15. A cauliflower is a tasty vegetable. 16. A doctor should be kind. 17. A child must play in the evening. 18. An army officer is very brave. 19. An airhostess looks after the needs of passengers. 20. An airforce pilot is very brave. 21. A computer is used to send e-mail messages. 22. A potato is a vegetable. 23. A policeman wears a cap. 24. A horse is a faithful animal. 25. An elephant is a big animal.

Exercise 3. My son studies in class 7. 2. My neighbours play their radio loudly. 3. The books that you bought me are lying on the table. 4. The sunflower is good for health. 5. The chairs are lying on the lawn. 6. The man whom you met at the station wants to see you. 7. The girl whose mother gave you a gift is waiting for you in the common room. 8. The apples were kept in the fridge. 9. The mice in the attic are a nuisance. 10. The children were waiting for you.

Exercise 4. He is a fine actor. (*countable*). 2. I want some milk. (*uncountable*). 3. We need oil. (*uncountable*). 4. There are four cats. (*countable*). 5. How much flour do you need? (*uncountable*). 6. We stayed in a hotel. (*countable*). 7. The bell is ringing. (*countable).* 8. We need to eradicate poverty. (*uncountable*). 9. The truth is that he didn't go anywhere. (*uncountable*). 10. I bought some coffee. (*uncountable*). 11. The keys are lying on the table. (*countable, countable*) 12. She has read this book recently. (*countable*). 13. Education is necessary for our development. (*uncountable, uncountable*). 14. History is an interesting subject. (*uncountable, countable*). 15. We have bought some coal. (*uncountable*). 16. I have already bought some eggs. (*countable*). 17. She is a student. (*countable*). 18 We must perform our duty. (*uncountable*). 19. She lit the fire with a match. (*countable, countable*). 20. Agriculture is very important for us. (*uncountable*).

Exercise 5. 1. We had a lot of fun on Diwali last year. 2. Delhi is the capital of India. 3. January is the first month of the year. 4. The Prime Minister visited Lucknow on Sunday. 5. I met Mr Sharma at the party in February. 6. During our visit to America, we went to see Lake Michigan. 7. Asia is the largest continent. 8. I took Rajesh to Dr Singh. 9. London is the capital of Britain. 10. Bill Clinton was once the President of the U.S.A. 11. Egypt is known for its pyramids. 12. We visited Europe last year. 13. Mohinder hit a century against Pakistan. 14. All of us visited Mr and Mrs Brown on Christmas. 15. Mount Everest is the highest mountain in the world.

Unit 4

Exercise 1. 1. women. 2. scarves. 3. dwarfs. 4. watches. 5. torches. 6. dresses. 7. deer. 8. leaves. 9. flies. 10. cities. 11. tigresses. 12. cargoes. 13. mattresses. 14. inches. 15. foxes. 16. boxes. 17. bushes. 18. loaves. 19. countries. 20. mice. 21. geese. 22. mosquitoes. 23. monkeys. 24. factories.

Exercise 2. 1. The books are in the bags. 2. I bought some/many torches yesterday. 3. We saw some/many oxen on the way. 4. We need some leaves for our practical classes. 5. There are some/many knives lying on the tables. 6. We saw some/deer in the zoo. 7. Those calves are very young. 8. The thieves were very cunning. 9. Tomatoes always turn red. 10. Heroes always love their country.

11. The children are playing outside. 12. I wanted some scarves. 13. She saw aeroplanes in the sky. 14. There were fish in the water. 15. She bought some/many dresses yesterday.

Exercise 3. 1. many tailors. 2. five men. 3. several bags. 4. ten taps. 5. many aircraft. 6. seven women. 7. the trees. 8. twenty tables. 9. many coats. 10. several ladies. 11. the churches. 12. six horses. 13. the clocks. 14. three doctors. 15. many knives. 16. fifteen handkerchiefs. 17. several pilots. 18. thirty pens. 19. several children. 20. many books. 21. several bottles. 22. several mangoes. 23. two crows. 24. many sheep. 25. several officers.

Exercise 4. *(The following are only some of the possible sentences)* 1. I gave her a bottle of milk/a cup of tea/a glass of juice, etc. 2. I bought a bar of chocolate/a bottle of milk yesterday. 3. I need a cup of tea/a bottle of ink. 4. There is a jar of honey/a piece of paper lying on the table. 5. She lost a piece of luggage. 6. Can you get me a cup of tea/a bottle of milk? 7. She wants a bar of chocolate/a jar of honey. 8. He drinks a glass of juice/a cup of tea. 9. Can you give me a piece of paper/a cup of coffee? 10. Would you have a cup of coffee/tea?

Exercise 5. 1. I met a smart boy yesterday. 2. I requested her to give me a glass of water. 3. I bought a loaf of bread from the corner shop. 4. She gave me a pot yesterday. 5. Radha wants a bottle/glass of milk. 6. There is a pen lying on the floor. 7. There is a piece of paper lying on the floor. 8. My mother gave my sister a piece of cake at breakfast. 9. My mother gave my sister an apple at breakfast. 10. Tom brought home a dog last night.11. Rasheeda wanted a cup of tea. 12. My father planted a tree in our house. 13. He put a litre of oil in his scooter. 14. She bought a bottle of jam yesterday. 15. She bought a book yesterday.

Unit 5

Exercise 1. 1. the cat's ear. 2. the grocer's shop. 3. Mary's house. 4. Salman's car. 5. The cat's paw. 6. Shakespeare's plays. 7. Sushma's book. 8. Menaka's purse. 9. Mr Tata's plane. 10. the lions' legs. 11. Dr Kapoor's factory. 12. the elephant's eyes. 13. the boys' cycles. 14. Lekha's marriage. 15. the children's toys. 16. the girls' frocks. 17. the teachers' room. 18. the women's saris. 19. the ladies' coats. 20. my brother's friend.

Exercise 2. 1. I was sitting in the front of the place. 2. Swati needs your mother's scooter. 3. What is the name of this theatre? 4. Where is your brother's car? 5. We liked the beginning of the movie. 6. I liked the President's speech. 7. The Principal gave me Maria's book. 8. Manoj's father is a doctor. 9. Paris is the capital of France. 10. The seats for the men are at the back. 11. The child was playing with the cat's tail. 12. Early morning is the best part of the day. 13. What is the meaning of this word? 14. We are afraid of the roar of the lion. 15. She is Elizabeth's sister. 16. The roof of the house is very strong. 17. We've kept the students' bags in the corner. 18. The children's books are kept in the corner. 19. The colour of your car is very attractive. 20. My brothers' houses were built in 1985.

Exercise 3. 1. My mother is a doctor. She goes to her clinic at 8 o'clock in the morning. 2. I met your aunt at the party last night. She was looking very healthy. 3. We saw a lion in the circus. It looked very ferocious. 4. Rakesh met the King of Spain at the Government House. He has invited him to Spain. 5. The bride looked very happy. She was accompanied by her brothers. 6. That woman is a policewoman. She lives in Gomti Nagar. 7. You've met my sisters. All of them live with my father. 8. We've bought five bulls/oxen. We have brought them from Haryana. 9. My father-in-law is a professor. He teaches in the English department. 10. His sons have joined the army. They are undergoing training in Chennai.

Exercise 4. *(Only the words to be used in the blanks have been given).* 1. mother/father. 2. nephew. 3. sister. 4. aunt. 5. heroine. 6. princess. 7. widower. 8. lionesses. 9. bulls/oxen. 10. tiger. 11. bridegroom. 12. mare. 13. daughter. 14. actress. 15. king. 16. waitress. 17. spinster. 18. hens. 19. father-in-law. 20. countess.

Exercise 5. *(Only the words to be used in the blanks have been given).* 1. She. 2. He. 3. She. 4. She. 5. She. 6. He. 7. She. 8. He. 9. She. 10. His. 11. His. 12. she. 13. he. 14. she. 15. she.

Exercise 6. *(Only the words to be used in the blank have been given).* 1. has. 2. are. 3. is. 4. has/have. 5. are. 6. have. 7. has/have. 8. is/are. 9. is. 10. has. 11. have. 12. is. 13. is. 14. is. 15. are.

Exercise 7. *(Only the words to be used in the blanks have been given).* 1. a pair of glasses. 2. a pair of trousers. 3. a pair of scissors. 4. a pair of binoculars. 5. a pair of pliers. 6. a pair of tights. 7. a pair of spectacles. 8. a pair of shorts. 9. a pair of forceps. 10. a pair of laces.

Exercise 8. *(Only the words to be used in the blanks have been given).* 1. are. 2. are. 3. They. 4. are. 5. are. 6. are.7. have. 8. They are. 9. are. 10. have.

Unit 6

Exercise 1. 1. a long train. 2. an airy room. 3. a table. 4. an ass. 5. a beautiful flower. 6. an ideal house. 7. a factory. 8. an old factory. 9. a very old factory. 10. a well decorated hall. 11. an extremely cold winter. 12. a very old man. 13. a man. 14. a bicycle. 15. an inkpot. 16. an umbrella. 17. an iron gate. 18. a brass gate. 19. an expensive coat. 20. a cat.

Exercise 2. 1. A young dog is very playful. 2. An old man can be active. 3. A man is mortal. 4. A leaf is green. 5. A bank officer works very hard. 6. A compact disc is very expensive. 7. A horse is a faithful animal. 8. An apple is good for health. 9. A student wears uniform. 10. An old computer is very cheap. 11. A red rose looks very beautiful. 12. A chair has four legs. 13. An orange tastes good. 14. An old house has big rooms. 15. A policeman wears a cap. 16 A duck is a bird. 17. A lion is a big animal. 18. An elephant has a big body. 19. An old novel can be an educative book. 20. A cheap watch does not last long.

Exercise 3. 1. Politicians should be sincere. 2. Hens are birds. 3. Oranges are delicious fruit. 4. Mice are afraid of cats. 5. Jet aeroplanes fly fast. 6. Children need to drink milk. 7. Cauliflowers are vegetables. 8. Computers can solve problems quickly. 9. Cricket players should have good health. 10. Mango trees give us shade. 11. Big towns sometimes are better than cities. 12. Trains run faster than buses. 13. Railway platforms are busy places. 14. Students should work hard. 15. FM radios have excellent reception.

Exercise 4. 1. Rakesh is a pilot. 2. She is a cook. 3. It is a tree. 4. It is a glass table. 5. Diana is a beautiful model. 6. He is a German. 7. She is a Canadian. 8. He is an IAS officer. 9. It is an excellent book. 10. He is a good doctor.11. She is an Australian. 12. He is a Chinese. 13. It is an ant. 14. Shefali is a university lecturer. 15. Varinder is a student. 16. It is a giant panda. 17. He is an Austrian. 18. She is a nurse. 19. He is a cricket player. 20. It is a folding chair.

Exercise 5. (Only *the articles to be used in the blanks have been given).* 1. a, the. 2. A, a, The. 3. A, a, a, The, the, the. 4. a, the. 5. a, The. 6. a, the. 7. a, the. 8. an, the. 9. a, The. 10. an, the, a.

Exercise 6. *(Only the words to be used have been given. If the blank does not require a word – is given).* 1. some. 2. –. 3. –. 4. some 5. a. 6. – – –. 7. some. 8. a. 9. the. 10. –. 11. –. 12. an. 13. a. 14. some, a. 15. some. 16. a. 17. some. 18. a, – . 19. –, the. 20. some, the.

Exercise 7. There was a knock on my door at 2 o'clock in the morning. I opened the door and found an old man standing at the door. He had a gun in his hand and a cigarette in his mouth. I didn't realise that there was a young man behind him. The old man pointed the pistol at me and the young man took out a piece of paper. He gave the piece of paper to me. I read it and realized that it was an arrest warrant to arrest one Mr Kalra. I told them that I was not Kalra and that they had come to the wrong house. The old man put the pistol in his pocket and the young man took back the arrest warrant from me. Both of them apologized to me and left my house.

Unit 7

Exercise 1. The moon revolves around the sun. 2. The table lying in the corner was made by my grandfather. 3. The Germans have developed the automobile industry. 4. Diana is the most punctual woman in our office. 5. I read the *Hindustan Times* in the morning. 6. My mother brought a dog last week but my father did not like the dog and gave it to our neighbours. 7. I need to see the Principal. 8. We went to see a play at the Prithvi theatre yesterday. 9. Rekha is the tallest girl in our class. 10. You can take the book with the blue colour. 11. The sun is shining. 12. I visited Shimla last year and stayed in the house where I was born. 13. The next meeting of the Board of Directors will be held in the Taj Palace Hotel. 14. The Japanese can be very friendly. 15. The Prime Minister will visit Chandigarh next month. 16. There is a boy and some girls in the hall. The boy is playing with a ball and the girls are playing badminton. 17. The lady in the red dress is a police officer. 18. The Canadians are good at playing hockey. 19. We stayed at the Clark Avadh, when we visited Lucknow last month. 20. Vinay is the second man to win this contest.

Exercise 2. *(Only the articles to be used in the blanks have been given. If the blank does not require any article – has been given).* 1. a, –, –. 2. a, a. 3. an, –. 4. a, –, –. 5. –, –, –. 6. –, –, –, –. 7. –, –. 8. –, an, –, –. 9. –, –, –, –. 10. –, –, –. 11. a, –. 12. –, a, –, –, –, –, –. 13. a, –. 14. a, –, –. 15. –. 16. –, a. 17. –. 18. –, –. 19. –. 20. –, a, –. 21. –, an, –. 22. –, –, –, a, a. 23. –. 24. –, a, a, –, – , –. 25. an, –, –, –.

Exercise 3. *(Only the articles to be used in the blanks have been given. If the blank does not require any article – has been given).* 1. a, a, the, The, the. 2. an, a, The, a. 3. the, the, the, the –. 4. –, the, –, a, a. 5. a, a. 6. a, –. 7. a, a, the. 8. the. 9. The, the, a, the. 10. –, the, a. 11 a, –. 12. –, –, –, a. 13. a, an, the. 14. a, the. 15. The, –, the, the. 16. a. 17. the. 18. The, a. 19. The, the, –. 20. the. 21. the. 22. the, an. 23. The. 24. –, –. 25. –, –, –, a. 26. the. 27. –, –. 28. –, the, a. 29. –, –, The, –. 30. –.

Unit 8

Exercise 1. *(Only the words to be used in the blanks have been given).* 1. some. 2. some. 3. some, any. 4. any. 5. some. 6. any. 7. some. 8. any. 9. any. 10. some. 11. some, any. 12. any. 13. some. 14. any. 15. some. 16. some. 17. any. 18. some, any. 19. some. 20. some. 21. any, some. 22. any. 23. some. 24. any, some. 25. any.

Exercise 2. *(Only the words to be used in the blanks have been given).* 1. someone/somebody. 2. something. 3. anywhere. 4. anything/anyone. 5. something. 6. anything. 7. anyone/anybody. 8. somewhere. 9. anyone/anybody. 10. anything. 11. anything. 12. something. 13. somewhere. 14. anywhere. 15. anything.

Exercise 3. *(Only the words to be used in the blanks have been given).* 1. some. 2. some. 3. anything. 4. some, any. 5. something. 6. any. 7. some. 8. any. 9. somewhere, anywhere. 10. anywhere. 11. any. 12. anyone/anybody. 13. anyone/anybody. 14. any, some. 15. some, some. 16. someone/somebody. 17. any. 18 any. 19. anything, anyone. 20. some.

Exercise 4. *(Only the words to be used in the blanks have been given).* 1. many. 2. much. 3. a lot of. 4. many. 5. many. 6. many. 7. many. 8. a lot of. 9. a lot of milk. 10. much. 11. a lot of. 12 much. 13. many. 14. a lot of. 15. much.

Exercise 5. *(Only the words to be used in the blanks have been used).* 1. a few. 2. little. 3. little. 4. little. 5. a little. 6. few. 7. a little. 8. A few. 9. Few. 10. a few. 11. little. 12. a few. 13. few. 14. a few. 15. little.

Unit 9

Exercise 1. 1. flies. 2. talks. 3. teach. 4. opened. 5. work. 6. ran. 7. danced. 8. wrote. 9. carries. 10. sang. 11. eat. 12. gave. 13. roared. 14. likes. 15. play.

Exercise 2. 1. tested. 2. worked. 3. laughing. 4. completed. 5. dancing. 6. fried. 7. coughing. 8 walked. 9. writing. 10 trying. 11. slipped. 12. received. 13. lives. 14. killed. 15. reached. 16. love. 17. passed. 18. stopped. 19. use. 20. needs.

Exercise 3. 1. wrote. 2. completed. 3. like. 4. reading. 5. goes. 6. cutting. 7. drives. 8. known. 9. started. 10. dancing. 11. hit. 12. began. 13. rises. 14. drinking. 15. costs. 16. ringing. 17. died. 18. left. 19. sleeps/slept. 20. broken. 21. gave. 22. paid. 23. sang. 24. rung. 25. began. 26. sitting. 27. stopped. 28. gone. 29. read. 30. sleeps/slept.

Unit 10

Exercise 1. 1. has been (VA), watching (VM). 2. have (VA) read (VM). 3. went (VM), were (VA) playing (VM). 4. had (VA) written (VM). 5. will be (VA) meeting (VM). 6. does (VA), like (VM). 7. has (VA), closed (VM). 8. will (VA), attend (VM). 9. is (VA), taking (VM). 10. had (VA), left (VM), reached (VM). 11. will (VA) travel (VM). 12. has (VA), watched (VM). 13. do (VA) know (VM). 14. did (VA), meet (VM). 15. am (VA) visiting (VM).

Exercise 2. 1. is. 2. was. 3. shall/will. 4. has. 5. were. 6. had. 7. are. 8. are. 9. have. 10. were. 11. has. 12. am. 13. had. 14. is. 15. shall/will. 16. has. 17. have. 18. will. 19. will, am. 20. have.

Unit 11

Exercise 1. 1. is, was. 2. is. 3. are. 4. is, is. 5. am. 6. are, are. 7. is. 8. is, was. 9. were, are. 10. is, was.

Exercise 2. 1. She has/has got a factory near my house. 2. They have/have got a brand new car. 3. I have/have got a beautiful dress. 4. She said that she had/had got a car when she was young. 5. Sarika and her husband have/have got a house in Chandigarh. 6. I have just got a letter from my uncle. 7. When I saw her, she had just got a new car. 8. I had just got the loan from the bank, when I received my appointment letter. 9. They have/have got a spare scooter. 10. She has/has got five books on Shakespeare.

Exercise 3. 1. I had a wonderful vacation last month. 2. We had a good lunch at the airport. 3. I shall have some sugar in my tea. 4. I have a headache. 5. I had a haircut yesterday. 6. I have a pain in the ankle. 7.They had had a lovely evening at the party. 8. They had a wonderful day in Shillong. 9. She has a bad cold. 10. We just had breakfast.

Exercise 4. 1. will (MA), be (VA) taking (VM). 2. could (MA), have (VA) written (VM). 3. has been (VA) reading (VM). 4. ought to (MA), respect (VM). 5. shall (MA), visit (VM). 6. may (MA), take (VM). 7. might (MA), be (VM). 8. should (MA), finish (VM). 9. may (MA), be (VA), sleeping (VM). 10. must (MA), go (VM). 11. was (VA), having (VM), visited (VM). 12. will (MA), rain (VM). 13. can (MA), see (VM). 14. had (VA) , left (VM), reached (VM). 15. should (MA), have (VA), received (VM). 16. met (VM), looked (VM). 17. goes (VM). 18. is (VM). 19. might (MA), come (VM). 20. has (VA), given (VM).

Unit 12

Exercise 1. 1. He goes to college by bus. 2. He/She wants to visit Amritsar next week as his/her son has to take the medical entrance test. 3. He/She drinks a lot of milk in the morning and then he/she exercises in the garden. 4. He/She often forgets things. 5. My sister loves eating fish. 6. My friend drives slowly. 7. He/She always washes his/her hands before meals. 8. A/The dog enjoys eating meat. 9. A/The horse always eats grass. 10. He/She goes to office by train but comes back home by bus. 11. He/She pays Rs 3000 per month as rent for his/her house. 12. My brother has mobile phones and often rings me up in the evening. 13. The boy in our room gets up at seven in the morning and has breakfast by eight. 14. This man works in my office. 15. My friend leaves for Mumbai next week. He/She always spends his/her vacation in another city. 16. He/She always wears new clothes on New Year's Day. 17. A baby always cries a lot. 18. His/Her child hates drinking milk but loves eating chocolates. 19. This girl often passes your house. 20. This man wears very colourful clothes.

Exercise 2. 1. They run very fast. 2. We go for a long walk in the evening. 3. They walk to college ever morning and look for their friends on the way. 4. Those boys play cricket very well. They play cricket every evening. 5. We often watch a film on TV in the evening. 6. They manage their accounts so well. 7. These chairs cost Rs 300. 8. They have their lunch at 1 pm. 9. They go to work by bus and come home on foot. 10. Those girls want to talk to you. 11. They sometimes go to sleep at midnight. 12. We know English well. 13. Babies need a lot of attention. They need milk four to five times in a day. 14. Lions roar loudly. 15. We drink a lot of milk in the evening.

Exercise 3. 1. begins, ends. 2. leave. 3. rises. 4. looks. 5. boils. 6. go. 7. play. 8. Pour, whisk. 9. describes. 10. remains. 11. wear. 12. drives. 13. turns. 14. reach. 15. writes. 16. passes, sends. 17. leaves. 18. starts. 19. looks. 20. are. 21. take. 22. sets. 23. rains. 24. walks, salutes. 25. play.

Exercise 4. 1. is putting on. 2. am writing. 3. am dying. 4. are travelling. 5. is watching. 6. are carrying. 7. is waiting. 8. are running. 9. is drinking. 10. are lying. 11. am eating. 12. is sitting. 13. is riding. 14. is weeping. 15. is swimming. 16. is singing. 17. are sleeping. 18. is cleaning. 19. are stopping. 20. is crying.

Exercise 5. 1. is playing. 2. is showing. 3. is studying. 4. is working. 5. is closing. 6. is waiting. 7. is knitting. 8. is raining. 9. is talking. 10. are always making. 11. is repairing. 12. is constantly singing. 13. is playing. 14. am visiting. 15. is always humming.

Exercise 6. 1. wear. 2. is arriving. 3. are staying. 4. practises, is practising. 5. is leaving. 6. starts. 7. goes, is resting. 8. works, is preparing. 9. are just discussing. 10. are leaving. 11. always speaks. 12. writes, is trying. 13. is singing. 14. is giving. 15. gives. 16. enjoy, is cooking. 17. see, is trying. 18. is knocking. 19. always carries, is carrying. 20. always forget.

Exercise 7. 1. is knocking. 2. is running. 3. contains. 4. own. 5. is reading. 6. is opening. 7. are improving. 8. is stopping. 9. dislike. 10. has. 11. smell. 12. is shaking. 13. are laughing. 14. is changing. 15. belongs. 16. tastes. 17. is nodding. 18. are working. 19. are running. 20. is growing.

Unit 13

Exercise 1. 1. visited. 2. sang. 3. played. 4. locked. 5. met. 6. made. 7. put. 8. slept. 9. cleaned. 10. wrote. 11. stopped. 12. liked. 13. sold. 14. saw. 15. obeyed. 16. cut. 17. knew. 18. bought. 19. travelled. 20. broke.

Exercise 2. 1. I last saw 'Sholay' when I was in class 10. 2. Shefali joined our college a fortnight ago. 3. Rahul went to the hostel last night. 4. I waited at the station till they arrived. 5. His wife cooked dinner while he was watching TV. 6. I began to learn French when I was in class 8. 7. Jane attended the meeting on Monday. 8. I joined this company a month ago. 9. They spent their vacation last year in Simla. 10. I/We travelled to Ooty by car. 11. I met her at the station. 12. She sold her car last month. 13. She ate apples slowly. 14. He drank milk in the morning. 15. My father bought this house last year. 16. She lost her watch at the party. 17. She kept the milk in the fridge. 18. She put the keys on the table. 19. I wrote this essay a week ago. 20. It broke while I was keeping it on the shelf.

Exercise 3. 1. have already seen. 2. have recently bought. 3. has resigned. 4. has worked. 5. have written. 6. has already spoken. 7. have been. 8. have recently seen. 9. has posted. 10. has met. 11. have typed. 12. have worked on. 13. has lived. 14. have just cleaned. 15. has just joined. 16. has driven. 17. have known. 18. has sent. 19. has recently become. 20. has just washed.

Exercise 4. 1. have never driven. 2. have not seen. 3. bought. 4. have not written. 5. married, have gone. 6. married, went. 7. got. 8. has recently got. 9. had. 10. have just had. 11. have joined. 12. went, have not been. 13. have never seen. 14. cleaned. 15. have recently cleaned. 16. gave, have not taken. 17. have not written. 18. left. 19. visited. 20. have recently visited.

Unit 14

Exercise 1. 1. have been working. 2. has been standing. 3. has been repairing. 4. have been cooking. 5. have been living. 6. has been playing. 7. has been barking. 8. have been running. 9. have been practising. 10. has been raining. 11. has been studying. 12. has been singing. 13. have been driving. 14. have been teaching. 15. have been sitting.

Exercise 2. She has been working hard all day. 2. He has been crying. 3. They have been playing cricket the whole day. 4. She has been watching TV all day. 5. It has been raining. 6. He has been waiting for you since morning. 7. They have been discussing your plan for two hours. 8. She has been running. 9. They have been driving all through the day. 10. He has been travelling since yesterday.

Exercise 3. 1. I've been living in this house since 1980. 2. The baby has been crying for an hour. 3. She has been working in the post office since 1995. 4. He has been reading the novel since last week. 5. They have been learning French for five years. 6. Ahmed has been studying for two hours. 7. Rohan has been playing cricket since 1996. 8. Mukesh has been flying planes since 1990. 9. It has been raining since Tuesday. 10. I've been swimming for an hour.

Exercise 4. 1. Mary has been teaching Shakespeare for four months. 2. Mary has taught two plays until now. 3. Parvez has been studying political science for three months. 4. Parvez has studied four chapters so far. 5. Manoj has been travelling around India for six months. 6. He has visited four states so far. 7. My brothers have been selling TV sets since they left college. 8. My brothers have sold more than a thousand TV sets since they left college. 9. They have been counting money since morning. 10. They have counted fifty bundles until now.

Exercise 5. 1. since. 2. for. 3. since. 4. for. 5. since. 6. for. 7. since. 8. for. 9. since. 10. for. 11. for. 12. since.13. since. 14. for. 15. since. 16. for. 17. since. 18. for. 19. since. 20. for.

Unit 15

Exercise 1. 1. She was leaving school when I saw her. 2. While I was crossing the road, she waved at me. 3. I entered the room while she was teaching her class. 4. She was driving her car when she saw the accident. 5. We were playing football all evening yesterday. 6. I was listening to the evening news when I heard a knock at the door.

7. They were playing cricket in the morning yesterday. 8. We were watching TV at 7.30 in the evening yesterday. 9. They were sitting in the library when the Principal called them to his office. 10. She was having her lunch when I went to meet her. 11. Monica jumped off the train while it was moving. 12. They burst crackers while we were studying. 13. We were walking home when it started raining. 14. He was teaching all evening. 15. He was playing piano all evening. 16. Bina was typing a letter when Dr Singh called her. 17. She cooked dinner while her husband was writing letters. 18. My mother was making cake when the lights went out. 19. They were sleeping all evening yesterday. 20. The phone rang while I was taking a bath.

Exercise 2. 1. Mukesh was reading a newspaper at 8.00 pm. 2. Anil was having breakfast at 8.45 am. 3. Shefali was driving her car to college at 9.15 am. 4. Meena was travelling by train at 9.20 am. 5. Rakhi was writing letters at 10.30 am. 6. Waheeda was teaching class 12 at 10.45 am. 7. Meenakshi was cleaning her flat at 11.30 am. 8. Rehman was attending a meeting at 12.30 pm. 9. Mukesh was having lunch at 1.15 pm. 10. Shefali and Waheeda were studying in the library at 2.30 pm. 11. Anita and Shailaja were washing clothes at 3.15 pm. 12. The Board members were discussing your plan at 3.45 pm. 13. Mrs Kapoor was writing letters at 5.00 pm. 14. The Sharmas were watching TV at 7.00 pm. 15. We were having dinner at 9.00 pm.

Exercise 3. 1. It began to rain while we were playing cricket. 2. She was watching TV when I phoned her. 3. The bus was going very fast when I saw him on his scooter. 4. Roma was writing letters when she heard a noise outside. 5. She fell down while she was crossing the road. 6. I made tea while he was sitting in the drawing room. 7. I saw her at the party. She was wearing a beautiful dress. 8. I saw small boats while we were landing at the airport. 9. When I went to his house, he was taking lunch. 10. The children were playing in the garden when they saw a strange dog. 11. He was talking to a client when he learnt that his mother had passed away. 12. They were doing their morning exercise when they saw clouds in the sky. 13. Meenakshi took our class while it was raining outside. 14. We were listening to the evening news when a cat entered the room. 15. They were shouting when the Principal entered the classroom.

Unit 16

Exercise 1. 1. They had already left home when I phoned them. 2. My daughter was very happy to visit the zoo because she had never seen a tiger before. 3. Rakesh was not in his office. He had gone to deposit money in the bank. 4. After we had eaten dinner, we went out for a walk. 5. I felt that I had seen him somewhere before. 6. The rain had already stopped when I reached Nainital. 7. We were surprised to know that he had built a large bungalow. 8. The public library was no longer open. It had closed down. 9. When I reached the bus station, I remembered that I had left my certificates at home. 10. I couldn't identify my car. It had been badly damaged. 11. She told me that she had met Radhika in the morning. 12. When we reached home, our mother had already prepared the lunch. 13. I realised that I had met her earlier. 14. They went home after they had taught their classes. 15. I didn't recognize my aunt. She had grown old.

Exercise 2. 1. She was very happy. She had got grade A in the final exam. 2. I reached the station late. The train had already left. 3. He had already left his office when I went to see him there. 4. Seema had just got out when I arrived. 5. I was late. The car had broken down on the way. 6. Waheeda couldn't drive the big car. She had only driven small cars earlier. 7. Rehman couldn't attend the party last night. He had gone to Delhi. 8. Nobody opened the door when I reached their house last night. Probably everyone had gone to sleep. 9. She didn't have lunch with me. She had already taken her lunch. 10. There was no food left when we reached their house. The party had already been over.

Exercise 3. 1. She went to college in the morning and came home in the evening. She looked very tired. She had been teaching in college the whole day. 2. When I saw her, Mukesh was driving his car. He had been driving his car since morning. 3. We played cricket for an hour. Then it started raining. We had been playing cricket for an hour. 4. When I entered the house, I heard the sound of the TV. Someone had been watching TV. 5. When I entered my office, I saw my secretary typing a letter. She had been typing the letter since morning. 6. My daughter looked very happy as she was reading *Oliver Twist.* She had been reading *Oliver Twist* since her vacation started. 7. Rehman started working in Aden in 1986. He was still working in Aden in 1996. Rehman had been working in Aden for ten years. 8. When I reached their house, they were eating lunch. They had been eating lunch for half an hour. 9. When I entered his office, I found that he was sleeping. He had been sleeping in his office all afternoon. 10. Two girls came into the classroom. They were all wet. They had been walking in rain.

Exercise 4. 1. We had been singing in the main hall for half an hour when the power supply was disrupted. 2. She had been washing clothes in the washing machine for an hour when I reached her house. 3. I was in the library for half an hour when I realised that I was in the wrong room. 4. Dr Kapur had been in England for a year before he got a job in a hospital. 5. Meenakshi had been waiting for me in the library for half an hour before I reached the library.

Unit 17

Exercise 1. 1. shall stage. 2. will be. 4. shall drop. 4. will buy. 5. shall sell. 6. shall send. 7. will take place. 8. shall attend 9. will get. 10. will definitely pass. 11. shall wash. 12. will go. 13. will be. 14. will write. 15. shall have.

Exercise 2. 1. We shall stay... 2. I shall pay... 3. I shall take... 4. We shall declare... 5. I shall go... 6. I shall show... 7. I shall have... 8. I shall take... 9. I shall just phone... 10. I shall have...

Exercise 3. 1. I'm going to take a bath today. 2. They're going to buy a new car. 3. I'm going to have eggs at breakfast today. 4. She's going to leave by the afternoon flight. 5. Rakhi's going to teach us today. 6. We're going to write a book on English grammar. 7. They're going to construct a school building. 8. I'm going to have my breakfast. 9. He's going to meet the Principal tomorrow. 10. We're going to have a meeting on Monday. 11. I'm going to leave this place in an hour. 12. The government's going to increase the taxes. 13. She's going to stay with her grandmother next month. 14. I'm going to visit Rekha on Friday. 15. We're going to read *David Copperfield*.

Exercise 4. 1. We're going to win the match. 2. It's going to be very hot this year. 3. We're going to reach Chandigarh in half an hour. 4. He's going to fail in the examination. 5. It's going to be a hit. 6. I'm going to be late for school. 7. He's going to fall into the manhole. 8. It's going to rain soon. 9. You're going to fall sick. 10. It's going to land at the airport soon.

Exercise 5. 1. is leaving. 2. are starting. 3. are going. 4. is playing. 5. am catching. 6. are preparing. 7. am meeting. 8. are having. 9. is getting. 10. am working. 11. is meeting. 12. are going. 13. are staging. 14. are staying. 15.is showing.

Exercise 6. 1. leaves. 2. begins. 3. starts. 4. reaches. 5. starts. 6. prepare. 7. begins. 8. opens. 9. am. 10. are.

Unit 18

Exercise 1. 1. He'll be sleeping at 3 o'clock. 2. I'll be watching TV after dinner. 3. He's dictating a letter to her in the morning. 4. We'll be playing football from 4.00 to 5.30 in the evening. 5. I'll be teaching when you come back. 6. She'll be working at 11 o'clock tomorrow. 7. We'll be cleaning the house tomorrow morning. 8. I'll be travelling next Sunday at this time. 9. They'll be typing your papers all through the day. 10. We'll be driving to Varanasi next Monday morning. 11. She'll be painting the house after lunch. 12. I'll be cooking lunch after returning from college. 14. We'll be baking biscuits in the afternoon. 15. I'll be washing utensils after the party.

Exercise 2. 1. I'll be spending a week in London. 2. We'll be holding the examination in the second week of May. 3. She'll be meeting us at the airport. 4. We'll be playing the football match on Monday. 5. I'll be signing all the letters in the afternoon. 6. The plane will be leaving in half an hour. 7. The train will be arriving in an hour. 8. We'll be giving rebate on all items from Monday. 9. They'll be having dinner in half an hour. 10. He'll be seeing you in ten minutes.

Exercise 3. 1. We will have constructed the house by the end of the month. 2. By the end of the next week, they will have completed their training. 3. He will have taken the examination by the end of May. 4. By the end of this week, I will have waited for ten weeks for this reply. 5. India will have become a great nation by the end of this decade. 6. She will have finished teaching us French by the beginning of the next month. 7. She will have stayed with us for four weeks by next Monday. 8. He will have spent all his money before the end of the holidays. 9. Next year, they will have been in India for five years. 10. By next May, he will have written his next book.

Exercise 4. 1. By tomorrow evening, my parents will have come back home. 2. By next December, we'll have completed our assignments. 3. By next Sunday, they'll have finished constructing the new building. 4. By the time I finish this book, I'll have spent a fortune on it. 5. By Monday evening, my brother will have reached Paris.

Unit 19

Exercise 1. 1. They have not/haven't finished the work. 2. Her brother is not/isn't an officer. 3. They are not/aren't very tall. 4. I am not watching TV. 5. She was not/wasn't running fast. 6. We have not/haven't purchased this house. 7. Asha and Vibha are not/aren't playing the piano. 8. Mira can not/can't fly a plane. 9. Mrs Kapur will not/won't teach us tomorrow. 10. We are not/aren't working right now. 11. Meena and Urmila have not/haven't spoken to me. 12. You must not/mustn't exercise in the morning. 13. She can not/can't speak French. 14. Rajinder and Mohit are not/aren't studying in the library. 15. They were not/weren't great singers. 16. I am not thirty years old. 17. We could not/couldn't see her from a distance. 18. I would not/ wouldn't do it. 19. Haridas has not/hasn't cooked the lunch. 20. She is not/isn't a teacher. 21. Bill and Tom were not/weren't late. 22. I am not very tired. 23. You must not/mustn't sleep outside. 24. Razia has not/ hasn't sung this song. 25. The flowers are not/aren't very attractive.

Exercise 2. 1. She does not/doesn't take tea in the morning. 2. I do not/don't eat rice everyday. 3. They did not/didn't go to the station in the morning. 4. Amitabh and Neeta did not/didn't play tennis yesterday. 5. Raghavan does not/doesn't run very fast. 6. She did not/didn't hit a century yesterday. 7. Our servant does not/doesn't cut vegetables in the morning. 8. We did not/didn't enjoy the movie. 9. She does not/doesn't speak Italian. 10. They do not/don't like mangoes. 11. We do not/don't work here. 12. He does not/doesn't sing well. 13. She did not/didn't construct this house. 14. They do not/don't go to office in the morning. 15. Rehman and Aziz did not/ didn't buy books yesterday.

Exercise 3. 1. My father doesn't work in a company. 2. They weren't running fast. 3. She didn't open the door. 4. My brother hasn't reached Hyderabad. 5. You mustn't work in the evening. 6. He isn't a bank manager. 7. The car wasn't expensive. 8. I am not taking rest. 9. Her brothers don't drive. 10. It isn't hot today. 11. Reena and Arvind haven't written this article. 12. My sister can't drive very fast. 13. She shouldn't work at night. 14. We didn't go on vacation last year. 15. It isn't raining outside. 16. We didn't visit Nainital last summer. 17. My sister hasn't purchased a car. 18. She wasn't speaking to my brother. 19. My uncle doesn't own this shop.

Unit 20

Exercise 1. 1. I don't have a pet cat. 2. She doesn't have a small refrigerator. 3. They didn't have a garage in their compound. 4. Vikram doesn't have a good memory. 5. They don't have excellent books. 6. She hasn't got a lovely garden. 7. Naresh didn't have a cat when he was young. 8. I haven't got a ticket with me. 9. Monica doesn't have enough books to make a library. 10. We don't keep a dog in our flat.

Exercise 2. 1. can't. 2. don't. 3. can't. 4. doesn't. 5. isn't. 6. don't, haven't. 7. am not. 8. haven't. 9. doesn't have. 10. am not. 11. doesn't. 12. didn't. 13. didn't. 14. didn't, wasn't. 15. doesn't. 16. isn't.

17. aren't. 18. doesn't have. 19. didn't. 20. didn't. 21. won't/will not. 22. can't. 23. can't. 24. don't. 25. aren't.

Exercise 3. 1. He has no money to give you. 2. I see her nowhere. 3. There are no books on the table. 4. There was no milk in the fridge. 5. They have no fans in the house. 6. Naresh has no free time. 7. She offered us nothing in the evening. 8. There were no servants in the kitchen. 9. He likes books with no sad endings. 10. I'm going to give him no books. 11. There is no coat in the cupboard. 12. I have no sugar in the house. 13. She received no letter yesterday. 14. My uncle can read nothing at night. 15. There are no vehicles parked in the porch.

Exercise 4. 1. There isn't any salt in the bottle. 2. He doesn't have any car in his office. 3. They don't have any books with them. 4. I don't have any stamps. 5. Rita doesn't have any brothers or sisters. 6. The little girl didn't have any cotton clothes. 7. There isn't any petrol in the scooter. 8. There aren't any mangoes in the basket. 9. Mrs Mehta didn't give us anything to drink in the evening. 10. I don't have any dogs in my house. 11. She doesn't have any more thread to give you. 12. There isn't anyone outside. 13. My sister can't read anything in the evening. 14. My mother hasn't put any sugar in the tea. 15. They won't/will not do any work today.

Exercise 5. 1. any. 2. no. 3. any. 4. no. 5. no. 6. any. 7. any. 8. no. 9. any. 10. no. 11. no. 12. any. 13. no. 14. no. 15. any.

Exercise 6. 1. She never watches TV. 2. I'm going nowhere. 3. She seldom speaks to him. 4. We hardly meet each other in office. 5. She said nothing. 6. I know nobody in this locality. 7. We scarcely meet our neighbours. 8. Our mother rarely visits us. 9. Mrs Kulkarni can hardly speak English. 10. We rarely eat out. 11. She never spoke to me. 12. I never drink tea in the morning. 13. Krishna spoke to nobody. 14. We could hardly sleep at night. 15. I seldom drive my car. 16. My father never goes to the cinema. 17. I seldom speak to him on the phone. 18. We've seen her nowhere. 19. Professor Kumar scarcely takes his lectures these days. 20. She's bought no apples.

Unit 21

Exercise 1. Is her mother an army officer? 2. Will the Principal be here tomorrow? 3. Has she written this book? 4. Are the children studying in the hall? 5. Could he go on leave next week? 6. Will my friend be staying with you? 7. Are the guests enjoying the music? 8. Has he a dog in his house? 9. Is she really ill? 10. Would they like an invitation to attend the party? 11 Are they on their way here? 12. Has he a sister? 13. Must she attend a lecture tomorrow? 14. Am I late? 15. Is she taking a bath? 16. Has he a vehicle? 17. Have they gone out? 18. Can he leave tomorrow? 19. Is Dr Arvind at home? 20. Was her mother a teacher?

Exercise 2. 1. Do they work in this office? 2. Did Radha finish reading this book yesterday? 3. Does he drive a car every morning? 4. Does she sing well? 5. Did she pay him the money to buy vegetables? 6. Does it take a lot of time? 7. Do Vanita and Pooja go to office by bus? 8. Did her father fly a plane on this route? 9. Did she go to Delhi on Monday? 10. Does Madhu teach children in the evening? 11. Do Sonu and his friend run five miles every morning? 12. Do they live in Hyderabad? 13. Did Professor Narayan retire last year? 14. Does she swim everyday in the evening? 15. Did Rakesh leave a message for her in the evening? 16. Do Nita and her husband often go for a walk in the morning? 17. Did Nitin receive the General Manager at the station? 18. Does Mona study in this college? 19. Does she run a mile everyday? 20. Did they attend her lecture in the afternoon?

Exercise 3. Are you reading a novel? 2. Does Seema sleep in the afternoon? 3. Has Farida already seen this film? 4. Did you meet her in college? 5. Do you like working in a bank? 6. Does Pamela have a dog? 7. Will Rohit watch TV tomorrow? 8. Were you late for the lecture today? 9. Can Meenakshi make a doll? 10. Did you live in the centre of the city in Mumbai? 11. Are you waiting for Prashad? 12. Can Swami teach you French? 13. Did you have a nice holiday? 14. Are they going out this evening? 15. Could you read Sanskrit when you were young? 16. Has Promilla already taken her lunch? 17. Are your parents going to London next month? 18. Is Mukesh a pilot? 19. Do you run five miles everyday? 20. Have you been to New York recently?

Exercise 4. 1. Is there a car outside? 2. Did she sleep well last night? 3. Does Mohini work in a bank/Has Mohini worked in a bank? 4. Have you been to Cochin? 5. Do they have a pet/Have they got a pet? 6. Are you married? 7. Does he like milk? 8. Did Ramesh break the window yesterday? 9. Is/Was your father a doctor? 10. Do you have a refrigerator? 11. Does it rain a lot in Simla? 12. Is Rekha very beautiful? 13. Are your parents tall? 14. Did you watch TV last Monday? 15. Does she have a dog in her house? 16. Did you meet Iqbal on Monday? 17. Have they finished working? 18. Does he live in the USA? 19. Has her uncle been a policeman? 20. Did Prabha go out last night?

Exercise 5. 1. Yes, I will; No, I won't. 2. Yes, he did; No, he didn't. 3. Yes, I have; No, I haven't. 4. Yes, they are; No, they aren't. 5. Yes, it is; No, it isn't. 6. Yes, she does; No, she doesn't. 7. Yes, I've been; No, I've not been. 8. Yes, she is; No, she isn't. 9. Yes, they did; No, they didn't. 10. Yes, I am: No, I am not. 11. Yes, she is; No, she isn't. 12. Yes, I will; No, I won't. 13. Yes, they do; No, they don't. 14. Yes, she was; No, she wasn't. 15. Yes, I would; No, I wouldn't. 16. Yes, he has; No, he hasn't. 17. Yes, I have; No, I haven't. 18. Yes, it is; No, it isn't. 19. Yes they did; No, they didn't. 20. Yes, they are; No, they aren't. 21. Yes, she is; No, she isn't. 22. Yes, I will; No, I won't. 23. Yes, they have; No, they haven't. 24. Yes, I do; No, I don't. 25. Yes, she is; No, she isn't.

Unit 22

Exercise 1. 1. Who. 2. Which. 3. Whose. 4. Who. 5. Which. 6. What. 7. What. 8. Who. 9. Which. 10. Which. 11. What. 12. Who. 13. What. 14. Who. 15. Which. 16. Who. 17. Who. 18. What. 19. Who. 20. Who. 21. Which. 22. Whose. 23. Whose. 24. Who. 25. What/Who.

Exercise 2. Who(m). 2. Who. 3. Which. 4. Which. 5. What. 6. What. 7. What. 8. Who(m). 9. Whose. 10. Who. 11. What. 12. Which. 13. Who. 14. Whose. 15. What. 16. What. 17. Whose. 18. Who. 19. Who(m). 20. Which. 21. Who. 22. Who(m). 23. Whose. 24. What. 25. What. 26. Who(m). 27. What. 28. Who(m)/What. 29. What. 30. Who.

Exercise 3. 1. Where have you kept my keys? 2. Why did she go to Delhi? 3. When do you get up in the morning? 4. Where has she gone? 5. How does he behave in class? 6. When can you teach me English? 7. When is the next train? 8. Where is my bag? 9. How has he done in the examination? 10. Why did you attend the meeting? 11. When did she study in this school? 12. Where is the car parked? 13. Where can I keep my clothes? 14. How have you done it? 15. When can I meet you? 16. Why did she shout at you? 17. When did you start acting? 18. Where is Raju? 19. How can I reach your home? 20. When will you open your shop?

Exercise 4. 1. When does she go to bed? 2. Why has he gone to Kanpur? 3. Where has he gone? 4. When did you start going to school? 5. When will Mrs Singh give the lecture? 6. Where does she live? 7. How does he go to work? 8. How does she wash her clothes? 9. How are you going to Hyderabad? 10. When did you meet her? 11. Where do they play football? 12. When do they play cricket? 13. Why does Tarun go to Indira Nagar? 14. Why did you give him money? 15. How does she behave now? 16. Where is she going (to) on Monday? 17. How is Vaibhav working these days? 18. When did Monica meet you? 19. When can the Director meet her? 20. Where would she like to work? 21. Why is Rekha going to Kolkata? 22. When does Robin go for a walk? 23. How has he done the exams? 24. When can I ring you up? 25. Where can I see her?

Exercise 5. 1. How much do you want for this scooter? 2. How much time do we have to get ready? 3. How big is your house? 4. How old is your car? 5. How much does this book cost? 6. How many students are there in your class? 7. How many cups of tea do you drink everyday? 8. How much water do you drink everyday? 9. How fast is this plane? 10. How tall is your brother? 11. How often do you go on vacation? 12. How far is the airport from here? 13. How many members attended the meeting? 14. How long was the programme? 15. How strong is this building?

Exercise 6. 1. How many people attended the marriage? 2. How much milk is there in the bowl? 3. How tall is her mother? 4. How often do you visit Visakhapatanam? 5. How many students are there in the English literature section? 6. How many metres/How long is that cloth? 7. How often are the Asian Games held? 8. How many slices of bread do you want? 9. How much does this book cost? 10. How many members attended the meeting? 11. How many cups of coffee do you drink in the morning? 12. How many bottles of coke are there in the fridge? 13. How many inches are there in a foot? 14. How old is that building? 15. How often do you meet her? 16. How much sugar is there in the bag? 17. For how many years/How long did she stay in England? 18. How good are her paintings? 19. How much time do you have to type this letter? 20. How high is this building?

Exercise 7. 1. What was she writing with? 2. Who(m) does this scooter belong to? 3. What are you thinking about? 4. Which hotel did you stay at? 5. What are they talking about? 6. Who is he talking to? 7. Which chair was she sitting in? 8. Which hotel are they going to stay in? 9. What did she wash the dishes with? 10. Who did you give the money to? 11. Which song was Avinash listening to? 12. What are you cutting the vegetables with? 13. Who did you dream about? 14. Who is Sadhana waiting for? 15. What are they laughing at? 16. Where is she from? 17. What are your friends playing with? 18. Who is Usha talking to? 19. Who is he working for these days? 20. Where is Mr Johnson from?

Exercise 8. 1. Whose book is this? 2. Who is reading the newspaper? 3. What did she give him in the morning? 4. Who has eaten the apple? 5. What are Vijay and Manoj playing in the ground?

6. Where are Naresh and Rita? 7. When did you meet my uncle? 8. When can I meet the Principal? 9. Why did they take their rain coats? 10. How old is your father? 11. How many pens did she give him? 12. How much water is there in the tank? 13. How often do you visit this temple? 14. How many members have already come? 15. How many boys are there in the classroom? 16. Who was Mohinder with? 17. Who is he interested in? 18. What is she looking at? 19. Who is the new physics teacher? 20. Which girl wants to meet the Principal? 21. Which bus goes to Ludhiana? 22. Who did she speak to in the morning? 23. What happened in the morning? 24. Who does he want to meet? 25. How does she behave now? 26. Where are they sitting? 27. Whose shop is this? 28. When will the new manager join for duty? 29. Why has she gone to Kathmandu? 30. How good was the lunch? 31. How often do you eat in this shop? 32. How much water do you need to have a bath? 33. How much flour is there in the bag? 34. What is she looking at? 35. Who/What was he afraid of?

Unit 23

Exercise 1. 1. isn't it? 2. doesn't it? 3. won't they? 4. isn't it? 5 doesn't she? 6. hasn't she? 7. didn't they? 8. isn't she? 9. hasn't he? 10. wasn't it? 11. don't you? 12. doesn't it? 13. can't we? 14. doesn't it? 15. wouldn't he? 16. haven't you? 17. wasn't she? 18. didn't he? 19. didn't he? 20. hasn't it? 21. isn't it? 22. didn't they? 23. aren't you? 24. won't it? 25. isn't he? 26. doesn't it? 27. doesn't he? 28. haven't they? 29. isn't she? 30. didn't you? 31. hasn't she? 32. mustn't we? 33. shouldn't she? 34. doesn't she? 35. didn't they?

Exercise 2. 1. is he? 2. can she? 3. did they? 4. have you? 5. will you? 6. does he? 7. is it? 8. is it? 9. could they? 10. need I? 11. should he? 12. were they? 13. is she? 14. did I? 15. do you? 16. was she? 17. does she? 18. have they? 19. has he? 20. has she? 21. is he? 22. was she? 23. does she? 24. do they? 25. will he? 26. are you? 27. does it? 28. do we? 29. could she? 30. were there? 31. does she? 32. did they? 33. is he? 34. did he? 35. is it?

Exercise 3. 1. won't/will you? 2. won't/will you? 3. will you? 4. shall we? 6. will you? 7. shall we? 8. shall we? 9. will you? 10. won't/will you?

Exercise 4. 1. wasn't it? 2. did he? 3. haven't you? 4. doesn't it? 5. can she? 6. will you? 7. shall we? 8. will you? 9. won't he? 10. aren't they? 11. does she? 12. could she? 13. won't/will you? 14. won't/will you? 15. didn't she? 16. isn't he? 17. shall we? 18. don't they?

19. couldn't she? 20. has she? 21. won't/will you? 22. didn't she? 23. will they? 24. haven't you? 25. aren't you?

Unit 24

Exercise 1. *(Possible adjectives are given)* 1. small. 2. pleasant. 3. beautiful. 4. tall. 5. friendly. 6. red. 7. old. 8. big. 9. happy. 10. interesting. 11. boring. 12. new. 13. elder. 14. pious. 15. fine. 16. old, warm. 17. old. 18. artistic. 19. busy. 20. blue. 21. new. 22. youngest. 23. young. 24. costly. 25. brown, old.

Exercise 2. 1. dark clouds. 2. elder brother. 3. big house. 4. fresh air. 5. new car. 6. expensive gift. 7. foreign languages. 8. expensive hotels. 9. long journey. 10. beautiful photographs. 11. old car. 12. high wall. 13. difficult problem. 14. heavy box. 15. dangerous turn.

Exercise 3. 1. morning. 2. music. 3. steel. 4. copper. 5. garage. 6. village. 7. cricket. 8. insurance. 9. entertainment. 10. brick. 11. chemistry. 12. apple. 13. iron. 14. tennis. 15. wire.

Exercise 4. 1. a little white metallic box. 2. the calm Western wind. 3. the new political party. 4. a black cat. 5. an English painting. 6. a heavy commercial vehicle. 7. a beautiful blue dress. 8. a new blue car. 9. an ugly green shirt. 10. the new agricultural equipment. 11. a red delicious Kashmiri apple. 12. the famous Victorian building. 13. the weak military regime. 14. an old Hindi movie. 15. the successful national party.

Unit 25

Exercise 1. 1. healthier. 2 . bigger. 3. tastier. 4. more modern. 5. softer. 6. more comfortable.7. better. 8. taller. 9. taller. 10. more polite. 11. more careful. 12. heavier. 13. more helpful. 14. bigger. 15. prettier.

Exercise 2. 1. Rani is taller than her sister. 2. Meera is more musical than Devi. 3. Delhi is hotter than Jammu in summer. 4. Her work is more careless than mine. 5. Her house is older than mine. 6. His room is colder than mine. 7. Monish is quicker than Naresh. 8. This house is bigger than that. 9. A car is more expensive than a scooter. 10. She was more famous than her brother. 11. Meenakshi is a better swimmer than her daughter. 12. My driving is worse than my wife's. 13. She is friendlier than her sister. 14. This sum is simpler than the sum given in the book. 15. This car is noisier than your car (yours). 16. Her father was more courageous than her uncle. 17. The major was braver than the captain. 18. My uncle is wiser than my aunt. 19. He is more reserved than his sister. 20. This iron bucket is heavier than that plastic bucket.

Exercise 3. 1. Lucknow is a little colder than Delhi today. 2. Rita is much older than her sister. 3. My father is much taller than my uncle. 4. Your room is a little bit wider than my room. 5. My uncle is much older than my aunt. 6. Rita's sister is much more meticulous than Rita. 7. Yesterday, I was much more tired. 8. This book is a little bit costlier than that book. 9. My brother is a little older than his wife. 10. A car is much costlier than a motorcycle.

Exercise 4. 1. the tallest girl. 2. the biggest state. 3. the most talented actress. 4. the most interesting book. 5. the best student. 6. the shortest boy. 7. the oldest building. 8. the most diligent girl. 9. the bravest officer. 10. the kindest lady. 11. the most practical man. 12. the most difficult problem. 13. the most courageous boy. 14. the fastest runner. 15. the most active worker.

Exercise 5. 1. He's the stoutest man I've ever seen. 2. She's the tallest girl I've ever met. 3. That's the whitest flower I've ever seen. 4. It's the most delicious cake I've ever eaten. 5. It's the easiest sum I've ever solved. 6. This is the most beautiful city I've ever seen. 7. This is the fastest train that I've ever travelled on. 8. Mr Kapur's the noblest person I've ever met. 9. You're the wisest man I've ever met. 10. This is the reddest chilly I've ever seen. 11. It's the tastiest food I've ever eaten. 12. It's the most wonderful dinner I've ever had. 13. Veena's the thinnest girl I've ever seen. 14. This is the best story I've ever read. 15. Rajan's the most generous person I've ever met.

Unit 26

Exercise 1. 1. interesting. 2. bored. 3. disturbing. 4. annoyed. 5. shocking. 6. terrified. 7. disturbed. 8. embarrassed. 9. terrifying. 10. tiring.

Exercise 2. *(Possible answers are given)* 1. This is a weekly magazine. (attributive) 2. I am not afraid of ghosts. (predicative) 3. My sister is very tall. (predicative) 4. This is a wonderful film. (attributive) 5. I'm answerable to the President. (predicative) 6. She was unwilling to do this work. (predicative) 7. The eastern army has been moved to the border. (attributive). 8. That is an occasional journal. (attributive). 9. I am glad to hear that. (predicative). 10. She was delighted to meet us. (predicative). 11. My aunt is very fond of me. (predicative). 12. He is incapable of doing anything. (predicative). 13. That thin girl is my niece. (attributive). 14. *The Times of India* is a daily newspaper. (attributive). 15. You're liable for this act. (predicative). 16. I am tired. (predicative). 17. My elder brother is a pilot. (attributive). 18. I was very anxious to reach home. (predicative). 19. I was pleased to know that she had passed the exam. (predicative). 20. This wide road goes to Chennai. (attributive).

Exercise 3. 1. She was shocked at his behaviour. 2. My father is good at playing cricket. 3. Monica is afraid of dogs. 4. The bag is full of sugar. 5. Vijay is interested in literature. 6. Lata Manageshkar is famous for airing so many songs. 7. She is incapable of doing anything. 8. My son is proud of standing first in the class. 9. Her daughter is upset for failing in the examination. 10. She is hopeless at drawing anything. 11. I am sorry (that) Nina doesn't have enough money. 12. You're late for your school. 13. He's not fit to do this work. 14. He was rude to the clerk. 15. They're anxious to know the news.

Exercise 4. 1. Mohan is afraid to open the door. 2. He is able to do it. 3. I am happy to know that she has passed the examination. 4. It is difficult to open this window. 5. It is stupid of her to have gone out in the cold without a coat. 6. I am unable to drive this car. 7. Karan is certain to pass this examination. 8. Avinash is slow to react. 9. Shailaja is foolish to spend so much. 10. She is careful to draw pictures neatly. 11. I am sorry to be late. 12. She was overjoyed to receive your letter. 13. He is eager to do this work. 14. He is reluctant to do this job. 15. We are sure to win the match.

Unit 27

Exercise 1. 1. well. 2. intelligently. 3. fast. 4. informally. 5. high. 6. strangely. 7. foolishly. 8. automatically. 9. quickly. 10. late. 11. bravely. 12. unhappily. 13. badly. 14. slowly. 15. gracefully.

Exercise 2. 1. She watches TV in the evening. 2. I saw her yesterday. 3. She'll come soon. 4. She gets up at 5 o'clock. 5. I'll ring her up tomorrow in the evening. 6. I can meet you on Wednesday in the afternoon. 7. I read this novel last month. 8. The examinations begin on 1st March. 9. I'll teach you Shakespeare now. 10. I'll reach Delhi (on) Friday morning. 11. She got the Filmfare award in 1992. 12. She arrived on Sunday night. 13. This house was constructed in 1931.14. He joined our/my office last year. 15. She's opening her shop next month.

Exercise 3. 1. already, must already. 2. just/already, still. 3. yet. 4. just, already. 5. anymore, recently. 6. anymore, recently. 7. recently, yet. 8. anymore. 9. still. 10. yet.

Exercise 4. *(Possible answers have been given.)* 1. I have just finished reading this book. 2. They're still playing football. 3. Have you already finished eating? 4. We watched this film last week/on Monday. 5. I read this book last year. 6. They played football in the evening. 7. This machine is still not working. 8. They've recently/already sold their house. 9. I met her here/outside/yesterday. 10. She left Mumbai in 1997/last year. 11. She's recently left Mumbai. 12. He is just now sleeping inside. 13. She is not teaching in this college anymore. 14. He doesn't work in this bank anymore. 15. She doesn't play hockey anymore/on Sundays.

Exercise 5. 1. I've recently/already seen this film. 2. Did you read *India Today* last week? 3. I read this newspaper today. 4. I didn't watch TV today. 5. I've spoken to him several times this week. 6. I wrote several letters this week. 7. He hasn't done anything this year. 8. She didn't withdraw the money from the bank today. 9. She hasn't cleaned her car this week. 10. We haven't got water today.

Unit 28

Exercise 1. 1. She sometimes visits us. 2. I have often visited this school. 3. I usually bring work from the office. 4. He has occasionally been writing a short story. 5. Monica always looks bright. 6. Do you usually work hard? 7. They have frequently been working late. 8. She almost always gets good marks in English. 9. She can occasionally be rude. 10. Have you always lived in this house?

Exercise 2. 1. She wasn't often late when she worked in our office. 2. She isn't usually at home in the evening. 3. He normally doesn't work in the afternoon. 4. They generally didn't complain about the hostel food. 6. She's sometimes not in office when I ring her up. 7. They don't sometimes play in the morning. 8. She wouldn't often finish the work in time. 9. She doesn't frequently reach home by 10 o'clock. 10. Trains aren't always very reliable.

Exercise 3. *(Possible adverbs/adverbials have been given).* 1. in the bathroom. 2. under the table/there. 3. out. 4. in the garden/at the airport. 5. near me. 6. in Pune. 7. in London. 8. in a bank. 9. on the table. 10. in the kitchen. 11. in our school. 12. in her room. 13. at the airport. 14. at the party. 15. in the living room.

Exercise 4. *(Possible adverbs have been given).* 1. quite. 2. quite/very. 3. very/extremely. 4. very much. 5. very. 6. rather, very. 8. fairly. 9. rather. 10. pretty.

Exercise 5. 1. very. 2. very much. 3. very. 4. too. 5. very much. 6. too. 7. very. 8. very. 9. very much. 10. too. 11. too. 12. very. 13. very. 14. very much. 15. too. 16. very much. 17. very. 18. too. 19. very much. 20. very.

Unit 29

Exercise 1. 1. My father can even sing/Even my father can sing. 2. My brother only passed the test/Only my brother passed the test. 3. Monica can even speak German/Even Monica can speak German. 4. She can only drive a car/Only she can drive a car. 5. He can even direct a film/Even he can direct a film.

Exercise 2. 1. Seldom do I go to Mumbai. 2. Little does Rakesh realise that it is very important. 3. Never have I done such a thing in my life. 4. Never will I visit her house again. 5. Barely can she lift this box.

Unit 30

Exercise 1. 1.We will not/won't play football this evening. 2. Fyaz can not/can't write interesting essays. 3. They may not visit us tomorrow. 4. She could not/couldn't finish her work on time. 5. You should not/shouldn't write to him. 6. You must not/shouldn't sit here. 7. They should not/shouldn't visit the hostel. 8. Renu will not/won't attend the class on Monday. 9. Vijay may not take your car. 10. He can not/can't attend my lecture today. 11. It will not/won't rain in the evening. 12. You must not/mustn't phone her. 13. They ought not to have done it. 14. She must not/mustn't write him a letter. 15. I could not/couldn't play football when I was a child.

Exercise 2. 1. Will Professor Kumar take our class tomorrow? 2. Could I meet you at the bus stand? 3. Will he go now? 4. Can I eat this piece of bread? 5. May we leave this room now? 6. Can you see me in the evening? 7. May I borrow your car? 8. Will you open the window? 9. Shall we watch the film? 10. Ought we to wait for some more time? 11. Can she go with you? 12. Will it rain tomorrow? 13. Must I do it now? 14. Can she make some tea? 15. May I see your garden?

Unit 31

Exercise 1. 1. He can drive a car. 2. Could I borrow your book? 3. You cannot/may not smoke here. 4. Rita can fly a plane. 5. Can I drive this car? 6. Rehman could attend the meeting yesterday as he took the morning train to Jabalpur. 7. She can walk ten kilometres every day. 8. You may go on leave next week. 9. Could I borrow some books from the library? 10. They could operate this machine, when they were young. 11. Could we take part in this discussion? 12. May we attend the conference? 13. He can/may participate in the national games. 14. You can borrow my car tomorrow. 15. You may not park your car here. 16. Can I use your telephone? 17. You may not smoke here. 18. My grandfather could not/couldn't swim. 19. You can not/may not travel in the first AC compartment. 20. Could I use your pen?

Exercise 2. Would you like a cup of tea? 2. Would you like an orange? 3. Would you like a chapati? 4. Would you like some juice? 5. Would you like some vegetables? 6. Would you like some potatoes? 7. Would you like some milk? 8. Would you like some dal? 9. Would you like a mango?

Unit 32

Exercise 1. 1. It may rain tomorrow. 2. He could/might be attending the meeting. 3. I might win the prize. 4. The best of pilots may make judgment errors. 5. Sunita may be in her office. 6. The state could/might be placed under the Governor's rule. 7. Debashish may visit Ahmedabad next week. 8. Kailash could/might be on his way to the bank. 9. The team may be preparing for the final match. 10. Our team could/might win the match. 11. The house may still be vacant. 12. Rita may pass the examination. 13. They might have been married. 14. The engine may work. 15. They could/might be listening.

Exercise 2. 1. He may/might/could be in his office now. 2. She may/might/could have watched TV yesterday. 3. He could/might have been at home yesterday. 4. Anita may/might/could be at home tomorrow. 5. The plane might/could have left Amritsar at 5 pm. 6. The plane may/might leave Amritsar at 5 pm. 7. They may/might open school at 8 o'clock. 8. They might have opened school at 8 o'clock. 9. She might have been playing cards in the afternoon. 10. She might have been sleeping at 4 o'clock. 11. He may/might be working today. 12. She may/might/could have left. 13. They may/might/could have finished work. 14. She may/might/could be in the library. 15. They may/might/could be in the office.

Exercise 3. 1. Can I read this book? 2. May I attend the French classes? 3. Shall we attend the prayer? 4. We could meet the Principal. 5. Would you have lunch with us tomorrow? 6. Will you switch on the television, please? 7. Shall we have dinner now? 8. Can I drink a glass of mango juice? 9. Could you lend me your car, please? 10. Could I meet the Principal? 11. May I borrow this book from the library? 12. Would you drop me at my hostel? 13. We could walk down to the market. 14. Will you shut the window, please? 15. May I discuss this issue with the Director? 16. Can I have some potatoes? 17. Would you switch on the fan, please? 18. Could I borrow your book? 19. Shall we start the meeting now? 20. Shall we go out for dinner tonight? 21. Can I drink/have some coke? 22. Could I have the salt, please? 23. Will you switch on the TV, please? 24. Would you show me that card? 25. Can we play cricket in the afternoon?

Unit 33

Exercise 1. 1. must. 2. had to. 3. had to. 4. must. 5. must. 6. have to. 7. must. 8. must. 9. have to.

Exercise 2. 1. You must submit the application today. 2. He should have/ought to have informed you that he should not meet you today. 2. He should have/ought to have informed you that he would not meet you today. 3. You must meet the doctor today. 4. Rekha should/ought to support her younger brother. 5. She must use glasses. 6. We should/ought to respect our teachers. 7. They should have/ought to have seen the Principal in the morning. 8. We must finish our work on time. 9. He should have/ought to have taken your permission before he took a week's leave. 10. Visitors should/ought to have parked their vehicles outside the gate. 11. You should/ought to have reported to work within ten days. 12. Students must wear their games uniform on Saturdays. 13. You must stop smoking. 14. You should/ought to stop smoking here. 15. She is in the hospital. You should/ought to go and see her there.

Exercise 3. 1. needn't. 2. mustn't. 3. mustn't. 4. needn't. 5. needn't. 6. mustn't. 7. needn't. 8. mustn't. 9. mustn't. 10. needn't.

Unit 34

Exercise 1. 1. main clause: He told me; subordinate clause: that the Prime Minster would visit Lucknow; conjunction: that. 2. main clause: I shall help you; subordinate clause: if you pass this examination; conjunction: if. 3. main clause: He noticed; subordinate clause: that he never attended the meeting; conjunction: that. 4. main clause: The fact is; subordinate clause: that he never attended the meting; conjunction: that. 5. main clause: . . . . . is unbelievable; subordinate clause: That the building has collapsed; conjunction: That. 6. main clause: I shall see you; subordinate clause: after I have finished the lecture; conjunction: after. 7. main clause: I couldn't see the Principal; subordinate clause: Although I reached the college at 9 am; conjunction: Although. 8. main clause: . . . . . . was known to everybody; subordinate clause: That she was coming; conjunction: That. 9. main clause: The rumour was; subordinate clause: that she had been dismissed; conjunction: that. 10. main clause: we went out for a walk; subordinate clause: As Shakti had returned early; conjunction: as. 11. main clause: We will go out; subordinate clause: when you are ready; conjunction: when. 12. main clause: You may leave the class; subordinate clause: as soon as you have finished your paper; conjunction: as soon as. 13. main clause: I last met him; subordinate clause: when he lived in London; conjunction: when. 14. main clause: I'll visit Delhi; subordinate clause: if you grant me leave; conjunction: if. 15. main clause: . . . . . . was expected by everyone; subordinate clause: That our team would win the match; conjunction: That.

Unit 35

Exercise 1. 1. That India won the one-day series did not come as a surprise to anyone. 2. That Kunal has stood first in the ISC examination has brought credit to the school. 3. That she will meet the President of the USA indicates her popularity in the international community. 4. That the troops have been withdrawn has not changed our government's policy. 5. That Rajinder was promoted as Lieutenant Colonel raised the morale of the battalion. 6. That America is a superpower is a known fact. 7. That India is the largest democracy is very creditable for us. 8. That he can speak English well will help him in passing the examination. 9. That she has become a pilot has come as a surprise. 10. That he had made a mistake was clear.

Exercise 2. 1. Kamlesh accepted that her sister had taken the book. 2. She told me (that) you were coming here on Tuesday. 3. I regret (that) she did not give me the discount. 4. Vikram dreamt (that) he had become a general. 5. We heard (that) you are going to the USA.

6. Sunita knows (that) Sridhar has passed the examination. 7. Ajay found (that) his house had been occupied. 8. They said (that) the taxes would not be increased. 9. She feels (that) we should buy a car. 10. The officer announced (that) there would be an increase in pay.

Exercise 3. 1. The chances are that we'll win the match. 2. The suggestion was that the meeting should be held after two months. 3. The assumption is that democracy will survive. 4. The decision was that Varoon would be given a scholarship. 5. My advice is that you should attend the interview tomorrow. 6. The answer is that you can join duty. 7. The feeling is that there should be no examination. 8. The news is that India has won the cricket match. 9. The hope is that we shall get the help. 10. The belief is that everyone is equal in democracy.

Exercise 4. *(Some possible sentences are given).* 1. It was sad that someone entered our house. 2. It is clear that we have to do it. 3. It is clear that Karishma has passed the examination. 4. It is obvious that we have to do it. 5. It is obvious that someone entered our house. 6. It is true that she never attends the meeting. 7. It is true that we have to do it. 8. It is obvious that Karishma has passed the examination. 9. It is good that Karisma has passed the examination.

Exercise 5. 1. I am disappointed that the incident occurred. 2. Mrinalini is certain that Rahul could do it. 3. Mrinalini is certain that she'll pay you the money. Mrinalini is certain that he'll win the prize. 4. Mrinalini is certain that she'll be selected. 5. She is astonished that Rahul could do it. 6. I am hopeful that she'll pay you the money.

Exercise 6. 1. It has surprised us that she has failed in the examination/That she has failed in the examination has surprised us. 2. He believed that she could do it. 3. She said (that) she could look into the matter. 4. It is good that she has come. 5. He told me (that) you were coming on Tuesday. 6. It was clear that he had made a mistake. 7. It is a fact that the earth is round/That the earth is round is a fact. 8. He was certain that you would attend the meeting. 9. I am confident that I can do it. 10. I feel (that) he should be given a raise. 11. The Principal announced (that) the exams would begin on 2nd April. 12. The assumption is that the inflation rate will not increase. 13. The fact is that we have paid all the instalments. 14. I am sorry that she behaved in such a manner. 15. It is true that she wrote this letter. 16. It was appreciated by everyone that Monica completed this work/That Monica completed this work was appreciated by everyone. 17. She knows (that) you'll attend the meeting. 18. Our advice was that they could start the degree in computer science. 19. She is glad that you attended her sister's marriage. 20. I dreamt (that) I had stood first in the exam. 21. It enhanced the reputation of our company that he was awarded Padma Bhushan/That he was awarded Padma Bhushan enhanced the reputation of our company. 22. I am hopeful that we'll get the aid. 23. It is important that you attend the meeting. 24. She assumed that you would attend the meeting. 25. The decision was that she would be promoted.

Exercise 7. *(Possible that-noun clauses have been given).* 1. that you were coming tomorrow. 2.that she has been promoted. 3. That the sun rises in the east. 4. that we started the meeting at 10 o'clock. 5. (that) you would vote for her. 6. that her great grandfather was a king. 7. (that) he was going to Mumbai. 8. (that) the match will be held on Tuesday. 9. that the oppsition will vote in favour of this bill. 10. that you have passed the exam. 11. That the government has revised the pay. 12. that Mohit is the best candidate for this post. 13. (that) she won't be able to teach us. 14. that the domestic gas process won't be hiked. 15. that he should be made the Managing Director. 16. That he became a Minister. 17. that she had met the President. 18. that we would get the loan. 19. that you join this course. 20. that she was very rude to you. 21. that Tuesday was a holiday. 22. that Rakesh would support the resolution. 23. That we voted in favour of the motion. 24. (that) Urmilla had got the M.B.A. degree from Imperial College, London. 25. that we should buy this property.

Exercise 8. 1. main clause: .... has thrilled everyone; that-noun clause: That she had become a pilot (used at the subject position). 2. main clause: The Minister announced........ ; that noun clause: that the bridge would be constructed within a week. (used as the direct object). 3. main clause: She feels.............. ; that-noun clause: that we should buy a vehicle. (used at the direct object position). 4. main clause:.............. is very creditable; that-noun clause; That India is the largest democracy. (used at the subject position). 5. main clause: The feeling is.............. ; that-noun clause: that there should be no examination. (used at the subject complement position). 6. main clause; The hope is.............. ; that-noun clause: that we shall get help. (used at the subject complement position). 7. main clause: Kiran is certain........... ; that-noun clause: that she will get this job. (used at the adjective complement position). 8. main clause: It is clear.............. ; that-noun clause: that he is not going to help you. (used at the delayed subject position). 10. main clause:.............. is no less than a miracle; that-noun clause: That his father is alive. (used at the subject position). 11. main clause: She is insisting........... ; that-noun clause; that we should pay an advance on the rent. (used at the direct object position). 12. main clause: Mohini suggested .... ; that-noun clause: that we should go on a vacation (used at the direct object position). 13. main clause: She is astonished .... ; that-noun clause: that Rahul could do it. (used at the adjective complement position). 14. main clause: I am convinced .... ; that-noun clause: that he is great writer. (used at the adjective complement position). 15. main clause: I am glad .... ; that-noun clause: that she has come. (used at the adjective complement position). 16. main clause: The reply is .... ; that-noun clause: that we should start the project. (used at the subject complement position). 17. main clause: The report is .... ; that-noun clause: that the interest rate has decreased. (used at the subject complement position). 18. main clause: We were hopeful .... ; that-noun clause: that she would survive. (used at the adjective complement position). 19. main clause: It is possible .... ; that-noun clause: that she has reached Delhi. (used at the delayed subject position). 20. main clause: The general has ordered .... ; that-noun clause: that the troops should move immediately. (used at the direct object position). 21. main clause: She assumed .... ; that-noun clause: you would attend the meeting. (used at the direct object position). 22. main clause: ... demonstrates her lack of social skills; that-noun clause: That she does not know him. (used at the subject position). 23. main clause: He told me .... ; that-noun clause: she was not right. (used at the direct object position). 24. main clause: The news is .... ; that-noun clause: that India has won the cricket match. (used at the subject complement position). 25. main clause: We are sorry ....; that-noun clause: that we could not call you back. (used at the adjective complement position).

Unit 36

Exercise 1. 1. I never believed what you told me. 2. She didn't know how Nasreen would respond to her question. 3. I know when she met him. 4. Can you remember where you have parked your scooter? 5. Tell me how you will manage. 6. I don't know why she didn't attend the party. 7. Mary asked me what time the train would arrive. 8. I can't tell why she arrived late. 9. I know why he didn't take the examination. 10. I'd like to know what he wants.

Exercise 2. 1. Can you tell me where the bank is? 2. Do you know what time the plane will arrive? 3. Tell me who Akbar's father was. 4. May I know when I can leave office? 5. I would like to know when you met her. 6. She knows how much it costs. 7. I wonder who's knocking at the door. 8. Do you know where Randhir lives? 9. I want to know what he wants. 10. Do you remember what time she left?

Exercise 3. 1. I don't know if he was present. 2. She asked me if Meena could stay with them. 3. Jivan asked her whether she had worked earlier. 4. I don't know if she is attending the meeting. 5. She asked me if I could drive a car. 6. I want to know if we should ring her up. 7. Tell me if she has finished her lecture. 8. Do you know if she went out alone? 9. She wants to know if you have a spare pen. 10. I don't know if she is coming to the meeting.

Exercise 4. 1. She asked me if Rita worked in that office. 2. I wonder if she will attend the meeting. 3. Ask him if he is ready. 4. Rani enquired if Hari had joined the company. 5. I don't know if he has played tennis today. 6. May I know if he has finished the book? 7. She asked him if he could come for dinner. 8. I asked her if she knew Rakesh. 9. I want to know if you can meet me tomorrow. 10. I wonder if she could help me.

Exercise 5. 1. main clause: He asked me........ ; subordinate clause: why I couldn't attend the party. (wh-clause). 2. main clause: I wonder........ ; subordinate clause: if she will meet you tomorrow. (yes-no clause). 3. main clause: I don't know ....; subordinate clause: when she will come. (wh-clause). 4. main clause: Could you tell me............. ; subordinate clause: where I can post this letter. (wh-clause). 5. main clause: I wonder .... ; subordinate clause: if he could lift that stone. (yes-no clause). 6. main clause: Mona enquired .... ; subordinate clause: whether the postman had come. (yes-no clause). 7. Main clause: Elizabeth asked me .... ; subordinate clause: when the meeting would end. (wh-clause). 8. main clause: I never believed .... ; subordinate clause: what you told me. 9. main clause: She asked me .... ; subordinate clause: if I could lend her my car. (yes-no clause). 10. main clause: Do you know .... ; subordinate clause: how much it will cost. (wh-clause).

Unit 37

Exercise 1. 1. The doctor who has his clinic in your building wants to meet you. 2. I work with the boy who is sitting with Rahul. 3. The lady who works in our library is Meenakshi's mother. 4. The boy who has stood first in school is my neighbour. 5. I am waiting for the girl who joined our school yesterday. 6. This is the girl who has been looking for you. 7. The director who has made this film has been selected for the National Award.

8. She is the girl who coaches our team. 9. The man who was waving at Anuradha is our Director. 10. The boy who is sitting in the front row asks a lot of questions.

Exercise 2. 1. The girl whom/who I had gone to meet was sitting in the chair. 2. The workers whom/who you wanted to meet have arrived. 3. The doctor whom/who you wanted to consult is available today. 4. The man about whom I was talking gave an interview on TV this morning. 5. The boy whom/who you teach at home is my neighbour. 6. My partner with whom I started my business has left for the USA. 7. The boy to whom she is going to be married is very thin. 8. These are the girls whom/who you wanted to meet. 9. The man with whom we stayed had two grown-up daughters. 10. I have selected the boy whom/who you had recommended.

Exercise 3. 1. Mohini works for a company that makes pens. 2. The car that Rakesh bought last year needs painting. 3. She owns a house that was constructed in the nineteenth century. 4. The dog that is chained to the door is very fierce. 5. The story that I was talking about appeared in this newspaper. 6.We live in an area that is threatened by floods every year. 7. I know the electronics shop that you want to visit. 8. I bought the sofa set that my wife liked. 9. The cat that I brought from Shillong has run away. 10. He liked the house that you wanted to sell.

Exercise 4. 1. The man whose daughter is your secretary wants to meet you. 2. The necklace that you gave me is very costly. 3. The inspector to whom you complained has been transferred. 4. He knows the person whom/who we have appointed as our manager. 5. The television set that we purchased last year is very good. 6. This is the man whose son is our college captain. 7. I've bought the book that you recommended to me. 8. The girl whose father gave you this bag is standing outside your office. 9. This is the dog whose owner has disappeared. 10. The lion that is roaring is very ferocious. 11. The doctor who saw you yesterday is on leave today. 12. The taxi by which we travelled to Kanpur had very comfortable seats. 13. The postman to whom you gave my letters knows me. 14. The people for whom we were waiting were late. 15. The people with whom we were staying were very nice. 16. This is the table that I want to buy. 17. The man whose house I'm purchasing is a doctor. 18. I'm quite annoyed with the boy who talks too much in the class. 19. The young lady who wants to interview you works for the *Times of India*. 20. The officer whose son has joined IIM, Kolkata wants to take us to lunch.

Unit 38

Exercise 1. 1. when. 2. why. 3. when. 4. where. 5. why. 6. when. 7. where. 8. when. 9. where. 10. when.

Exercise 2. 1. I know a place where you can get excellent food. 2. This is the time when we can start our new business. 3. That is the house where I was born. 4. The reason why I could not visit you was I did not remember your address. 5. There is a store in the corner where you can buy apple juice. 6. This is the shop where you can get good suits. 7. 1950 was the year when India became a Republic. 8. The bank where I work also deals with foreign exchange. 9. Do you remember the day when we went to school? 10. The office where my wife works is at the corner of the street.

Exercise 3. 1. My sister, who lives in Delhi, is a pilot. 2. We stayed at the Taj Hotel, which is a beautiful building. 3. I went to see Professor Nigam, who lives in Nehru Enclave. 4. Munira works for an electronic company, which makes TV sets. 5. Our driver, who is usually on time, was late today. 6. The girl over there, whose name I don't remember, is in our hockey team. 7. The new college building, which has fifteen big halls, will be opened next week. 8. Next month I'm visiting Mumbai, where my brother lives. 9. I often go to the stadium, which is only two miles from my house. 10. Mr Sharma, whose car broke down in the morning, has gone to office on scooter today. 11. Rakesh, whose mother is your college doctor, was with me in the law school. 12. I went to see the General Manager, who asked me to go to Chandigarh. 13. She introduced me to her youngest son, who is a captain in the army. 14. Our college principal, who has written four books on English grammar, has been nominated for the President's medal. 15. Veena told me her telephone number, which I wrote down in my notebook.

Unit 39

Exercise 1. *(Only the adverbial clause to be used in the blank has been given).* 1. when I saw you car. 2. as soon as/when you reach the station. 3. After he had his lunch. 4. when I met her last time. 5. While I was reading the newspaper. 6. While I was in Delhi. 7. When Mr Agnihotri died. 8. after they've finished this project. 9. after we've taken our exams. 10. After he had his dinner. 11. till I return. 12. After you pass your MBA. 13. before the rain starts. 14. When I first saw him. 15. after he came back from the USA.

Exercise 2. *(Only the adverbial clause of reason to be used in the blank has been given).* 1. because she likes him. 2. As Rajesh is the captain. 3. as it was raining. 4. As I knew my temper. 5. As/Since I was late. 6. because you have to get up early tomorrow morning. 7. As I had completed the work. 8. because/as she needs your help. 9. because he wanted to meet me. 10. As Farida is the eldest.

Exercise 3. 1. She behaves as if she were a queen. 2. I felt as if I was going to faint. 3. Mukesh talks as though he were a politician. 4. She looked as though she had not slept for days. . 5. Rehman hits the ball as if he were a tennis player. 6. Amitabh looked at Meenakshi as if he were in love with her. 7. Monica danced as though she had been a dancer. 8. John sang as if he had been a great singer. 9. She felt as if she had a fever. 10. Her dress made her look as though she had come to a party.

Exercise 4. 1. They built a garage so that they could park their car in it. 2. The University has raised the fees to pay higher salaries to professors. 3. I studied hard in order to get a good grade. 4. He took the umbrella so that he might not get wet. 5. The policeman went by car to meet the inspector. 6. Harsharan reached the railway station at 5 am to catch the first train to Chennai. 7. They have gone to the temple to pray. 8. Write two pages everyday in order to improve your handwriting. 9. I rang up the school to find out about my result. 10. She acted in my new film to gain experience in art films.

Exercise 5. 1. I have taken leave/so that I can write/to write a book on English grammar. 2. Ramesh has gone to Delhi to get a visa to Australia. 3. Gayatri left last night in order to catch the late night flight to Kolkata. 4. I met the Principal in the morning to discuss the new English syllabus. 5. He visited the General Manager to get a new telephone connection. 6. I gave her my car to go to Kanpur. 7. Rupali drove the car fast to/in order to/reach Vijayawada in time. 8. He went to the police station to complain against his neighbour. 9. Sudha went to the public telephone booth in the evening to ring up her uncle in Delhi. 10. I bought this shop to/inorder to/open a provision store.

Exercise 6. 1. Mrs Dhillon bought this house so that she could open a school. 2. The General Manager went to Delhi by the afternoon flight so that he could see the Chairman in the evening. 3. Mr Sharma built a strong iron gate so that his dog would remain inside the building. 4. I have cooked food so that you can eat it at lunch. 5. He worked very hard so that he could finish the work by Monday. 6. I've opened the tap so that you can fill water for the day. 7. They keep the windows open at night so that they can get fresh air. 8. Radhika has gone on long leave so that she can finish her Ph.D. 9. I've given him the key to my house so that he can/will stay there tonight. 10. The office order is typed in English and Hindi so that all the employees can understand it.

Exercise 7. *(Only the correct tense of the verb has been given).* 1. was travelling. 2. was. 3. will not meet. 4. was. 5. reach. 6. was. 7. reached. 8. returned. 9. was crossing. 10. has not written. 11. became. 12. lived. 13. was coming. 14. will serve. 15. was coming.

Exercise 8. *(Only the correct tense of the verb has been given).* 1. exercises. 2. are wearing. 3. is. 4. had passed. 5. am going. 6. drove. 7. use/have used. 8. was raining. 9. is. 10. never spoke.

Exercise 9. *(Only the correct tense of the verb has been given).* 1. were. 2. were. 3. suffered. 4. had been. 5. were. 6. had been. 7. had not understood. 8. had. 9. had never taken. 10. were.

Unit 40

Exercise 1. *(Only the correct form of the verb has been given).* 1. go. 2. will be paid. 3. heat. 4. will become. 5. go. 6. want. 7. will attend. 8. will take. 9. have. 10. go.

Exercise 2. *(Only the correct form of the verb has been given).* 1. would give. 2. were; would make. 3. had given. 4. knew; would read. 5. would not go. 6. got up. 7. would be. 8. had. 9. would get. 10. worked. 11. would tell.12. would invest. 13. were. 14. would not do. 15. knew.

Exercise 3. 1. would have reached. 2. would have survived. 3. had taken. 4. would have visited. 5. would have continued. 6. had bought. 7. would have won. 8. won. 9. would have caught. 10. would have entered.

Unit 41

Exercise 1. 1. He offered to drive her car. 2. I want to become a doctor. 3. Rakesh promised to finish the work by evening. 4. She tried to wash the car. 5. I refused to apologise to her. 6. You forgot to turn off the fan. 7. He failed to pass the driving test. 8. He learned to sing. 9. I hope to join college next year. 10. He can't afford to buy a scooter.

Exercise 2. 1. Rakesh advised me to work hard. 2. I asked her to paint a picture. 3. Our manager ordered us to work till 8 o'clock. 4. The soldier warned us not to cross the fence. 5. She invited Rakhi to watch TV. 6. Meera told Vinod to wait for her. 7. The doctor advised me to stay in bed. 8. Hari persuaded me to take up this job.

9. Mrs Kaul reminded us to finish our assignments. 10. I told him not to wait for me. 11. I reminded her to ring you up. 12. She told me not to close the door. 13. The librarian allowed me to sit in the library. 14. His father taught me to play cricket. 15. You didn't tell her to cook lunch.

Exercise 3. 1. She is very keen to meet you. 2. He is sure to pass the examination. 3. It is fun for us to watch this film. 4. She was very happy to meet you. 5. It was clever of him to solve the difficult sum. 6. It was foolish of him to ignore your letter. 7. It would look rude or us to ring them up now. 8. It was good of her to help you. 9. I was careful not to disclose your secret to her. 10. She is sorry to bother you. 11. It is difficult for us to climb the mountain. 12. It is hard to believe it. 13. Shefali was very glad to know that you were coming. 14. He is free to leave this job. 15. It was wicked of her to use such words.

Exercise 4. 1. She told me not to leave the library. 2. He was happy to have finished the work. 3. My son was delighted to learn that he had passed the entrance examination. 4. She was sorry to have missed the meeting. 5. It seems to have rained here. 6. She hopes to finish this novel by tomorrow. 7. I asked her to close the door. 8. She promised to give me the book. 9. She warned him not to drive. 10. Our officer ordered us to exercise in the open. 11. She reminded me to catch the early morning train. 12. She asked me to deliver the lecture in the evening. 13. They would be surprised to meet you. 14. I am sorry to have gone so soon. 15. He was hurt to learn that she had not done his work. 16. She didn't expect you to come. 17. She promised to take the children to the zoo. 18. He was hurt to learn that he had failed. 19. She would be surprised to see you. 20. She hopes to become a pilot.

Unit 42

Exercise 1. *(Only the gerund to be used in the blank is given).* 1. Reading. 2. playing. 3. writing. 4. Shouting. 5. raining. 6. Running. 7. Ridng. 8. riding; running. 9. swimming. 10. eating. 11. Turning. 12. writing. 13. painting. 14. Washing. 15. disturbing. 16. Eating. 17. eating. 18. working. 19. cooking. 20. Cooking.

Exercise 2. *(Only the pronoun to be used in the blank is given).* 1. him. 2. his. 3. my. 4. me. 5. her. 6. her. 7. them. 8. their. 9. you. 10. your. 11. him. 12. his. 13. you. 14. your. 15. her. 16. her. 17. him. 18. his. 19. you. 20. your. 21. us. 22. our. 23. you. 24. your. 25. her.

Exercise 3. *(Only the words to be used in place of brackets have been given).* 1. eating. 2. her snoring. 3. shouting. 4. your smoking. 5. walking. 6. her watching. 7. your telling. 8. your working. 9. having.

10. reading. 11. jumping. 12. my sitting. 13. her writing. 14. his leaving. 15. sleeping. 16. their coming. 17. meeting. 18. speaking. 19. opening. 20. returning.

Unit 43

Exercise 1. *(Only the words to be used in the blanks have been given).* 1. of; your driving. 2. of taking. 3. for being. 4. on joining. 5. in working. 6. in finding. 7. on giving. 8. of buying. 9. of going. 10. on giving. 11. to meeting. 12. of becoming. 13. for interrupting. 14. like going out. 15. at learning. 16. with working. 17. in teaching. 18. about/at going. 19. about flying. 20. for; ringing; me.

Exercise 2. *(Only the words to be used in the blanks have been given).* 1. helping him. 2. eating hot food. 3. working hard. 4. passing the examination with an 'A' grade. 5. sending her flowers. 6. for not sending you books. 7. writing letters. 8. watching TV in the evening. 9. speaking rudely to you. 10. receiving him at the station. 11. attending your wedding tomorrow. 12. entering the old house. 13. crossing the flooded road. 14. making a century. 15. singing. 16. taking a bath. 17. getting up early in the morning. 18. going to the seaside. 19. buying me a cycle. 20. stealing her dress.

Exercise 3. 1. Driving fast. 2. shouting. 3. ironing. 4. Being. 5. Running in the morning. 6. her singing. 7. Riding. 8. Flying planes. 9. disturbing you. 10. repairing TV sets. 11. leaving early. 12. making dolls. 13. Swimming in the morning. 14. swimming in the evening. 15. Cutting metal. 16. Sleeping late. 17. working for us. 18. Reading novels. 19. Her shouting. 20. getting up early. 21. Travelling by train. 22. travelling by train. 23. cleaning. 24. Teaching for six hours. 25. Their singing.

Exercise 4. 1. He went home after buying some potatoes. 2. She rang up her mother on reaching the airport. 3. He had dinner with his neighbours before going to the railway station. 4. She was taken to hospital after being hit by a car. 5. Monica went to England without meeting her parents. 6. Open the door without disturbing him. 7. My father sent me money after receiving my letter. 8. He got 'A' grade without working hard. 9. I realised I had left the ticket at home on reaching the airport. 10. Leena met her husband before passing the B.A. degree.

Unit 44

Exercise 1. 1. opening. 2. watching. 3. to travel/travelling. 4. to understand. 5. to know. 6. to visit. 7. to visit/visiting. 8. eating. 9. to paint. 10. to address. 11. watching. 12. getting up. 13. playing. 14. to play. 15. taking.

Exercise 2. 1. to read. 2. taking. 3. writing. 4. to play. 5. playing. 6. to lose. 7. to go. 8. shopping. 9. travelling. 10. listening to.

Exercise 3. to stop; playing. 2. to take; walking. 3. her asking; to meet. 4. taking; to eat. 5. to have. 6. reading; to watch. 7. knocking; to inform. 8. to become. 9. him to start; preparing. 10. trying; to steal. 11. my asking; to close. 12. to say; you to leave. 13. to meet. 14. you to study. 15. to finish; to remind. 16. to know; to visit. 17. to open. 18. her trying; to cross. 19. to remind; to switch off. 20. cooking; her refusing; to cook. 21. to leave; to speak. 22. your speaking; requesting; to expedite. 23. telling; to prepare. 24. raining; driving. 25. being; reading/to read.

Unit 45

Exercise 1. 1. Mohan said, 'I am going to Delhi tomorrow.' 2. 'It's lying on the table,' said she. 3. 'Are you keeping well,' Ramesh asked. 4. 'Drive as fast as you can,' said Sunita. 5. 'What a beautiful day it is!' she exclaimed. 6. 'Where were you?' he asked me. 7. 'We saw this film last week,' John said. 8. Meera said to me, 'I saw you last night.' 9. 'I saw you last night,' Meera said. 10. Meenakshi asked me, 'Who showed you my house?' 11. Rajan said, 'He is not keeping well.' 12. 'He is not keeping well,' said Rajan. 13. 'What's the time?' Gopal asked. 14. Gopal exclaimed, 'What a fool I've been!' 15. 'Shall we leave now?' she asked. 16. Farida asked, 'Is that his car?' 17. 'What a surprise!' he exclaimed. 18. Rehman said, 'I was sleeping in the evening.' 19. She exclaimed, 'What a lovely house you have!' 20. She said, 'Please take me to my father.'

Exercise 2. 1. She says that she has already read this novel. 2. Mary says that Sadhana is sitting in the library. 3. He says that he has typed those letters. 4. Captain Singh says that he's flown that plane for five years. 5. Monica says that you've a wonderful house. 6. She has just told me that the Prime Minister has arrived at the airport. 7. She says that she's very sorry. 8. He has just told me that they have already finished the work. 9. My mother says that I can call my friends next week. 10. She's always telling people that she drives very well. 11. Mr Kapur says that he works 12 hours a day. 12. Karan has just told me that his father is a cabinet minister. 13. Tanya says that she's got many friends. 14. She says that Meera is coming to the party. 15. He says that he's not feeling well.

Exercise 3. 1. Kunal told me that he'd go to Ahmedabad the following week. 2. He said that he could have helped me. 3. She said that she was living in Amritsar. 4. Monica told me that she had been sitting in her room. 5. Rakesh said that she hadn't finished her homework. 6. She told me that I should work hard. 7. He told me that he would see me the next day. 8. She told me that she had finished reading that novel the previous week. 9. Anima said that she didn't know what she'd do. 10. Vinod told me that I could go with him. 12. He said that he had kept it there in the cover the previous week. 13. The teacher told me that he'd/she'd teach me Shakespeare the following week. 14. Farida said that she was going to buy a new house. 15. Kunal said that he had woken up at 6 o'clock the previous day. 16. Punit said that they had come back to the hostel very late the previous day. 17. She said that the film was very interesting. 18. He said that he had not been well the previous day. 19. Ashish said that that book was very expensive. 20. Mohinder said that he had slept for four hours in the afternoon.

Exercise 4. 1. The officer said that she had to join duty the next day. 2. She told me that if she went to Chennai, she'd get a shirt for you. 3. Meera said that she had waited for me/you/till six in the evening. When I/you/hadn't turned up, she rang up my/your/home. 4. Avinash told me that when he reached the station, he found that the train had already left. 5. The clerk told me that all the trains for Varanasi ran in the evening and therefore I could buy my ticket in the afternoon. 6. The doctor told me that I had gained ten kilos and I was not doing any exercise in the morning. 7. The shopkeeper told me that he could get me the best quality sugar the next day/the following day and that I might take it in the evening. 8. My father said that I had to work hard if I wanted to join the civil services. 9. The officer said that he had caught him/me/her/red-handed and he/I/she/was saying that he/I/she/hadn't crossed the red light. 10. The new clerk told me that he had worked in the railways for five years but had to leave because he couldn't have travelled fifteen days a month. 11. My brother said that the film that he had seen the previous day had been an award-winning film. 12. Sarika told Anita that it was very hot in Lucknow in summer. Therefore I should have visited Lucknow in November. 13. Monish said that if I felt cold, he'd close the window. 14. Pradip said that the plane would leave in twenty minutes; so I should have left then. 15. Asha told me that as Nilofer had left Mumbai the previous day, she should have reached Guwahati the next day.

Unit 46

Exercise 1. 1. She enquired if I had studied hard for the exam. 2. Vinayak asked me if I had seen that film. 3. Ramesh wanted to know if I always travelled by car. 4. Mohini asked Rita if she would teach us Shakespeare the following year. 5. I wanted to know if Kamini had ever been to Kashmir. 6. She asked me if I had written that article. 7. Rohan asked her if it was raining outside. 8. Meenakshi asked him if he would attend office the following/next day. 9. Damini asked Sharda if she had visited Chandigarh the previous year. 10. Karan asked Varoon if he could use his car. 11. The English teacher asked me if I had seen Manohar the previous day. 12. She asked me if I was enjoying myself. 13. Sushmita asked Abhishek if he had chained the dog. 14. Hari asked me if he could take leave the next day. 15. Ashi wanted to know if she had switched off the fan before leaving the room. 16. Garima wanted to know/asked me if I was watching TV. 17. I wanted to know if Karishma had accepted that assignment. 18. My father asked me/wanted to know if I would take Roomi to the doctor. 19. Mira asked her husband if he was going to Lucknow the next day. 20. My neighbour asked me if I could hear a noise.

Exercise 2. *(Possible answers have been given).* 1. He wanted to know when dinner would be ready. 2. Mohini asked Rekha why she was crying. 3. I enquired how I could reach the port. 4. She asked me where I had kept the box. 5. Akram enquired how she would reach there. 6. Faryal enquired of them where they had gone the previous week. 7. Mala asked me when I could send the books to her. 8. Rahul enquired what I/he/she/ was looking for. 9. He asked me when I would come again. 10. She asked me why I hadn't spoken to her mother. 11. Manu wanted to know where they lived. 12. Vijay asked me how my mother was. 13. Hema wanted to know where she had kept her spectacles. 14. Ashok asked me how long I had worked in that office. 15. She enquired how far the airport was from the city. 16. He asked me what I had told my father. 17. My father asked me when I wanted him to reach the station. 18. She wanted to know how much that cap would cost. 19. He asked me who I was looking for. 20. He wanted to know how much it weighed.

Unit 47

Exercise 1. 1. She asked him to get her a glass of water. 2. She requested him to close the window. 3. The doctor advised the patient not to take cold water. 4. The English teacher warned Ajay not to enter the room. 5. Anshu asked Nirupama not to play loud music in her room.

6. He reminded me to send an e-mail to Arjun. 7. Rajneesh requested me to carry that box in my car. 8. He told me not to wait for him. 9. The teacher asked the class to open the book on page seventy two. 10. She warned him not to do that again. 11. My mother told me to wash my hair. 12. He asked me to wait there till he came. 13. Monisha requested me to give her my mobile. 14. Rohan advised me not to eat that rice. 15. The air hostess requested me to keep the aisle seat vacant. 16. He told me not to boil the tea. 17. The commanding officer ordered the Captain to fire at once. 18. The officer commanded the soldier not to leave for his platoon the next day. 19. The teacher asked the students not to make a noise. 20. My father told me to take the car out of the garage.

Exercise 2. 1. She asked whether she should help him/She wanted to know whether to help him. 2. She asked him if/whether she should cook the lunch/She wanted to know whether to cook the lunch. 3. Meera asked me if/whether she should get the car for me/Meera wanted to know whether to get the car for me. 4. Madhu asked me if/whether she should invite her to lunch/Madhu wanted to know whether to invite her to lunch. 5. Tanya asked Karan if/whether she should give him the letter then. 6. He asked whether she should heat that then/He wanted to know whether to heat that then. 7. My wife asked me if/whether we should start then/My wife wanted to know whether to start then. 8. She asked her husband if/whether she should bake the cake the next day/ She wanted to know whether to bake the cake the next day. 9. He asked me if he should close the door/He wanted to know whether to close the door. 10. Seema asked Akash if/whether they should meet the next day/Seema wanted to know whether to meet the next day.

Exercise 3. 1. Anita told me that she didn't know the way to the City Plaza. She further requested me to ask the traffic policeman the way. 2. The teacher asked the student why he hadn't done his homework. He further asked the student to go and report to the class teacher. 3. She asked me if I was coming to college the next day. He told me that everyone wanted to meet me. 4. My sister said that she was very thirsty and requested me to get her a glass of water. 5. My mother told me that she was very tired and wanted to know if she should wash the utensils the next day. 6. He asked me if I had got any soap and said that he wanted to have a bath. 7. Shailaja asked Vijay where he had put the book and further told him that she wanted to study English literature. 8. My father asked me to go to the post office and post those letters. He further told me that those letters had to reach his branch office the following week. 9. Kunal asked Vishal if he would have dinner with them the next day. He told him that they were having a party the next day. 10. The officer ordered the soldier to take the jeep to the airport and bring the Commanding Officer there. He further informed/told the soldier that he would wait for him in the mess. 11. She told me that she was going to the station and enquired whether she should buy my ticket also. 12. My mother told her friend that the shops closed at 8 o'clock and asked if they should go to the market then. 13. He asked me when I was leaving for Delhi and said that she wanted to give me a small packet for her mother. 14. Nora told Ali that she usually went to the office by bus and asked if he took the morning bus to the office. 15. She told me that she had gone to sleep at 10 o'clock the previous day and said that she didn't remember when I returned home. 16. The Principal told me that he wanted me to join the debating club and asked me to see Mr Kapoor the next day. 17. My friend requested my father if he could speak to Harish and further told him that he was speaking from Mumbai. 18. The shopkeeper enquired if he might help me/him/her and further said that they had got some fresh dry fruit that day. 19. He asked me if I had ever been to Chandigarh and further said that it was a very beautiful city. 20. Rohit requested Raju to get him some medicines and told him that he was not feeling too well that day.

Unit 48

Exercise 1. *(Only the passive forms of the verbs have been given).* 1. are required. 2. was opened. 3. will be discussed. 4. were invited. 5. will be staged. 6. was hit. 7. is hit. 8. was taken. 9. will not be published. 10. were not sold. 11. will be declared. 12. were taught. 13. are checked. 14. is not opened. 15. was inaugurated. 16. will be inaugurated. 17. is not allowed. 18. was killed. 19. will not be disturbed. 20. will be repaired.

Exercise 2. 1. Breakfast is served (by her) at 7 o'clock. 2. This novel was read by Meera last week. 3. The results will be declared (by the university) next week. 4. My pen was stolen from my pocket. 5. Lunch is cooked (by my mother) in the morning. 6. This dish was cooked (by the cook) yesterday. 7. A pair of socks will be knit for you (by her) next week. 8. The food was burnt by my sister last night. 9. The vegetables were cut into pieces. 10. This car was hit (by a truck) last night. 11. These letters will be posted (by us) tomorrow. 12. The thief was caught (by the police) at the railway station. 13. His first novel was published when he was twenty-five. 14. We were taught English by Mrs Nancy in class 11. 15. This office is opened at 9 o'clock. 16. The rent was not paid (by them) for two years. 17. Arabic is spoken in more than twenty countries. 18. The shop will not be opened tomorrow. 19. The food was not cooked yesterday. 20. Flowers are regularly planted in the garden.

Unit 49

Exercise 1. 1. are being questioned. 2. is being parked. 3. is being made. 4. are being withdrawn. 5. are being distributed. 6. are being cut. 7. is being washed. 8. are being taken. 9. is being boiled. 10. is being interviewed.

Exercise 2. 1. was being pulled. 2. were being cancelled. 3. were being counted. 4. was being sung. 5. was being cooked. 6. was being staged. 7. was being discussed. 8. was being cut. 9. were being marked. 10. was being served.

Exercise 3. 1. The house was being cleaned in the evening. 2. The case is being opened again. 3. A documentary film was being made when I reached the studio. 4. Food is being cooked (by her) on the lawn. 5. The students are being taken on a picnic by bus. 6. Food is being served in the main hall. 7. Tickets were being distributed at the entrance. 8. Loud music was being played at night. 9. Clothes are being washed in the garden. 10. Shirts are being ironed with a steam iron. 11. The report cards were being prepared in the morning. 12. A new market is being built near the bus stand. 13. Potatoes were being fried when I entered the kitchen. 14. New letter pads are being printed. 15. Our car was being cleaned (by the driver) when we reached home.

Exercise 4. 1. A new tax rate has been announced (by the government). 2. The front door has been broken. 3. This film has already been screened. 4. The photographs had already been shown to us when you telephoned her. 5. Two houses have been recently built (by them) near our house. 6. My scooter has been stolen. 7. The evening mail has already been delivered. 8. This story has already been heard *(though the active is preferred here)*. 9. The murder mystery has been solved (by the police). 10. The house had been struck by lightning before we reached there. 11. They had already been warned (by us) before you came with the court notice. 12. This latest novel has been published by Rushdie. 13. The dinner has already been cooked. 14. The building had been painted. 15. Fifty workers were employed to build the road. 16. The door has been opened (by her). 17. The train has been stopped. 18. The house has been demolished. 19. The meals have already been prepared. 20. The parade has been viewed (by the Prime Minister) *(though the active is preferred here)*.

Exercise 5. 1. You'll be driven to the station *(though the active is preferred here)*. 2. The law must be obeyed. 3. A book on tribal languages must have already been written. 4. Such a pen can be bought anywhere. 5. The thief might have been caught (by the police) by now. 6. She must have already been received at the airport. 7. This mystery cannot be solved. 8. The test could have been successfully conducted last month. 9. The meeting will be conducted tomorrow.

10. She must be taken to the doctor. 11. My watch must have been stolen while I was standing at the bus stand. 12. This house should not be bought (by them). 13. Every rupee must be accounted for. 14. The door could have been opened in the evening. 15. The clothes must have been collected.

Exercise 6. 1. I was asked a question in the class. 2. He will be given the book tomorrow. 3. We were taught French in class 9. 4. She was recommended to another doctor. 5. The plumber has already been paid his monthly wages. 6. We were told (by our English teacher) to attend the class on Sunday. 7. Kamlesh was requested to deliver a lecture on Wednesday. 8. She has already been given permission for the journey. 9. I was allowed (by the Principal) to take the examination again. 10. The guests were shown the new college building. 11. They were asked a difficult question. 12. Vinod was given enough money (by her) to visit Japan. 13. Each girl will be allowed to wear her personal clothes once a week. 14. He can be asked to proceed on leave. 15. He has been given a new project.

Unit 50

Exercise 1. *(Only the forms to be used in the blanks have been given).* 1. It is expected. 2. It is hoped. 3. There is said. 4. Rakesh is thought. 5. There is believed. 6. It is hoped. 7. It is known. 8. There is supposed. 9. The gang is thought. 10. It is feared. 11. The Head is known. 12. It is thought. 13. Radhika is considered. 14. India is supposed. 15. It is believed.

Unit 51

Exercise 1. 1. in. 2. at. 3. at. 4. in. 5. in. 6. on. 7. at. 8. on. 9. in. 10. on. 11. at. 12. in. 13. on. 14. on. 15. on. 16. in. 17. at. 18. in. 19. in; in. 20. in. 21. at; in. 22. on. 23. at. 24. in. 25. at. 26. in; on. 27. in. 28. in. 29. at. 30. in.

Exercise 2. 1. into. 2. to. 3. into. 4. to. 5. to. 6. into. 7. into. 8. onto. 9. into. 10. into. 11. to. 12. to. 13. onto. 14. to. 15. to.

Exercise 3. 1. above. 2. over/under. 3. beside. 4. below. 5. beside. 6. above/below. 7. under/beside. 8. behind. 9. beside. 10. under/beside/on. 11. over. 12. under. 13. behind/beside. 14. below. 15. behind/beside.

Unit 52

Exercise 1. 1. at. 2. at. 3. in; in. 4. in. 5. in. 6. in; on. 7. in. 8. at. 9. on. 10. at; in. 11. in. 12. on. 13. in; in. 14. in. 15. in. 16. on. 17. in. 18. at. 19. in. 20. at. 21. in. 22. at; in. 23. on. 24. at. 25. in.

Exercise 2. 1. for. 2. during. 3. during. 4. for. 5. during. 6. during. 7. for. 8. for. 9. during. 10. during.

Exercise 3. 1. until/till. 2. until/till. 3. by. 4. by. 5. until/till. 6. by; until/till. 7. by. 8. until/till. 9. by. 10. until/till.

Unit 53

Exercise 1. 1. by. 2. with. 3. with. 4. by. 5. with. 6. by. 7. by. 8. with. 9. by. 10. by. 11. by. 12. by. 13. with. 14. by. 15. by.

Exercise 2. at. 2. in. 3. on. 4. into. 5. to. 6. in; in. 7. by. 8. above. 9. by. 10. on. 11. in. 12. in; in. 13. in; for. 14. over. 15. under. 16. below. 17. at. 18. by. 19. during. 20. to; by. 21. behind. 22. during. 23. during; in. 24. at. 25. in. 26. at/by. 27. until/till. 28. to; by. 29. until/till. 30. onto. 31. in. 32. on. 33. behind/beside. 34. during. 35. on. 36. during. 37. by. 38. with. 39. to; on/until/till. 40. with.

Unit 54

Exercise 1. *(Only the phrasal verbs to be used have been given. In some sentences you may have to make other changes).* 1. set in. 2. get along. 3. turn up. 4. fell out. 5. dropped out. 6. fell apart. 7. stayed up. 8. Hold on. 9. stood out. 10. passed away. 11. made off. 12. settled down. 13. fell through. 14. broke down. 15. fall off. 16. dozed off. 17. went on. 18. come down. 19. dragged on. 20. broke out. 21. dropped in. 22. have not caught on.

Exercise 2. 1. pulled down/knocked down. 2. stepped up. 3. crossed out. 4. wiped out. 5. fixed up. 6. drawn up. 7. cooked up. 8. make up. 9. brought up. 10. handed over. 11. set aside. 12. fill in. 13. hushed up. 14. take down. 15. tried out. 16. sort out. 17. see off. 18. carried out. 19. fill up. 20. look up. 21. give up. 22. brought out. 23. phase out. 24. ruled out. 25. messed up.

Exercise 3. 1. looked into. 2. fell for. 3. bank on. 4. laughed at. 5. counting on. 6. disposed of. 7. looked after. 8. to get over. 9. called on. 10. broke into.